King Ahab – or Falk and Jenny

A novel by

Matti Isachsen Aikio

Translated by John Weinstock
Introduction by Gunnar Gjengset

Agarita Press

Set in Minion Pro

The original of this book was published as

Kong Akab

Roman
Alexander Brandts Forlag
København 1904

Cover design by John Weinstock and Beth Brotherton

Ollu giitu dáid olbmuide hui buori veahki ovddas:
Reidar Rødland, Harald Gaski,
Gunnar Gjengset, Elina Helander-Renvall.

This translation has been published with
the financial support of NORLA.

King Ahab – or Falk and Jenny

JOANNIS SCHEFFERI
ARGENTORATENSIS

LAPPONIA
Id est,

REGIONIS LAPPONUM
ET GENTIS NOVA ET
VERISSIMA DESCRIPTIO.

In qua multa

De origine, superstitione, sacris magicis,
victu, cultu, negotiis Lapponum, item Animalium, me-
tallorumque indole, quæ in terris eorum proveniunt,
hactenus incognitæ

Produntur, & eiconibus adjectis cum cura illustrantur.

FRANCOFURTI
Ex Officina CHRISTIANI WOLFFII
Typis JOANNIS ANDREÆ.
ANNO M. DC. LXXIII.

Matti Aikio's King Ahab – an introduction

by

Gunnar Gjengset, Phil. Dr.

Matti Aikio, or Mathis Isachsen as he originally called himself, was born in Karasjok on June 18, 1872. His parents were the sacristan and mayor Mathis Isachsen (1827-1904) and Ragna Heimo (1835-1912). He was a Sámi author who wrote in Norwegian at a time when the position of the Sámi people in Norway was under threat, and his books and depictions of Sámi life were widely perceived as caricatures of the Sámi people. This introduction will challenge such an opinion.

As his father was a sacristan, and therefore under the circumstances a schooled man, he provided a good foundation for young Mathis to enter a county school in Vadsø in 1888. Here he showed such good abilities that in 1890 he received one of two seats available for Sámi at a teacher's training college in Tromsø. And, by the way, the very same college where I started my career as a lecturer, 90 years later. This was Aikio's first meeting with the Norwegian language in a learning situation, and he graduated in 1892. He then worked one year at a primary school in Tana.

In spring 1896, he became Norway's first registered Sámi student. For a while he studied law, but abandoned his studies and worked as a high school teacher at a private school from 1903 to 1904, until his debut as an author with his novel *King Ahab - or Falk and Jenny*, which was published in Copenhagen in 1904. He made his Norwegian debut with the novel *In Reindeer Hide* in Kristiania (Oslo) in 1906. It was with this release he changed his name to 'Matti Aikio'. He chose a paradoxical position, having emerged as a Sámi in a particularly assimilation-prone, newly independent Norway. He adopted the more Sámi-like name Aikio, which he obtained from the Finnish branch of his family. One year later his novel *Ginunga Gap* was released, and in 1911 his fourth book, *Son of the Hebrew*, hit the market. It was translated into German in 1914. In the same year Aikio issued a collection of articles, short stories, poems and humorous pieces in *Letters from the Polar Land and Others*, which also contained two stories about Lars Levi Læstadius and one larger article about the Kautokeino Rebellion in 1852.

His novel *The Chapel of the Herdsmen* was released in 1918. And only in 1929 was his last novel published, *The Village at the Riverbend*. Aikio's strong interest in visual arts, and especially sculpture, resulted in a presentation of the sculptor Gustav Vigeland, especially his fountain works, with a booklet in the book series Norwegian artists in 1920. Matti Aikio was a man with artistic energy. He gave no explanation for why he chose to leave Karasjok, one of the central areas for Sámi culture, language and way of life in the Northern Hemisphere, other than the fact that he earned schooling opportunities as a reward for his general aptness. Nor did he explain why he chose to become an artist rather than an academic, or specifically why he chose a profession as an author rather than a career as a visual artist.

Apart from the information that he was descended from a long line of particularly skilled sled builders in Karasjok, it's hard to find clues to explain his selection of an artist's career anywhere in his letters or manuscripts. His obvious admiration for the sculptor Gustav Vigeland and Aikio's modest exhibition at Blomquist Antiquarian as a sculptor in his own right in 1926, might otherwise indicate he would want to become a visual artist. He was among other things also a competent newspaper cartoonist.

With his first book *King Ahab – or Falk and Jenny* from 1904, Aiko presented a main character who was skilled both as a scholar and an author – and as an acceptable suitor for a woman from the upper class. In contrast to the white man's ideas about the Sámi people, the author wanted to present Falk as most likely a Sámi. By withholding such information from the other characters in the book, the author shows that this ethnic relationship was discriminated against during the period. We must assume that the author thereby wanted to confront this disciminatory attitude.

The composition indicates this was done after careful deliberation. As far as the action and plot are concerned, it was not imperative that the main character might possibly be a Sámi: this is knowledge the narrator shares only with the author and the reader. Aikio could have refrained from doing this; he might have been writing about the insurmountable social barriers in the Swedish province of Norway, published under the name of the Norwegian author Mathias Isachsen. But he played with his Sáminess, took the pen name Aikio and asserted that ethnicity did not stand in the way of becoming an author. *King Ahab – or Falk and Jenny* is a book about injustice and forgiveness that seeks to mediate far too broad a social chasm, where the subtext is about ethnic antagonisms. The book is written by an author who gives the presentation a somewhat disjointed perspective, but one which works towards an identity theme. This coincides with the author's construction of his own identity through his choice of his own name.

By the year that followed Norwegian independence in 1905, the Sámi people along the coast were already socially déclassé. In the social stratification along northern Troms and the Finnmark coast at that time, Norwegian settlers and fishermen-farmers constituted the highest social stratum, while Kvens and Sámi competed at the lowest levels. The Kvens, immigrants from Finland, had a higher ranking than the Sámi in the new capital-based fishing industry, while Norwegians had a monopoly on the automated whaling industry. The settled and farming Sámi in Aikio's home town of Karasjok were now put under pressure in Norwegian public life. One can only speculate as to whether Matti Aikio sensed he was dancing on hot coals when he wrote about the Sámi people's destiny at a time when society as a whole had in fact just sealed that very destiny. But this notwithstanding, Aikio – albeit after careful consideration – included descriptions of how even seemingly well integrated Sámi could also rebel in his next novel *In Reindeer Hide*, should this prove necessary. There is no doubt that the author was obliged to make some delicate choices with respect to his methods, if he were to sell any books about the Sámi at all to the ultra-xenophobic, contemporary Norwegian population. For this reason, Aikio's compositions were often experienced as divided: through total assimilation, the colonized culture meets its end. Simultaneously, the colonizer wants to be segregated, with unforeseeable consequences. The text therefore also emphasizes that racial antagonisms must be overcome by cultural means: in relation to the "Germanic race," the "Mongolian races" (the Sámi) have nothing to offer. But one must stand up for ones culture. Aikio therefore sets up a cultural practice amidst an ethnically mixed Sámi population to counter the colonizer's hegemony. The Sámi people want to herd reindeer; the Norwegians want trade and industrious citizens. The core region for the realization of Sámi culture is in the mountains, but in symbiotic contact with the village and in mutual cooperation with the Norwegian trading villages along the coast. Here the Sámi and Kvens compete for positions in the middle and lower classes. Aikio had a good understanding of these groups' common ethnicity, and maintained that a better attitude towards integration here would serve to smooth the social antagonisms in play. Otherwise, they would disappear into the title of a novel that he began writing immediately after the release of *In Reindeer Hide*, namely *Ginunga Gap*.

No doubt, Matti Aikio wanted to put on display this white whale that swam around in the depths under the Europeans' mythical notions about Ultima Thule. Up against the white man's perceptions of the Sámi, Aikio presented one main character in *Kong Ahab* who was qualified both as an academic and an author – and as an acceptable suitor for a woman from the upper classes. The author wished to display him probably as a Sámi, while he also presented himself as a Sámi. By disclosing this knowledge for the other players in the text, the author shows that such ethnic relations were off limits at the time. We must therefore assume that the author wanted to confront this discriminatory attitude.

At the same time, Matti Aikio was busy staging himself: he had tried studies and teaching jobs, he wrote articles in the papers, but it seems as if he realized in the end he was an artist. Facing a potential publisher he emphasized his Sámi origin and flirted deliberately with contemporary needs for exoticism. Sámi culture was, and is, the otherness of northern areas, and here Aikio was far ahead of the first Inuit writer Mathias Storch and the Finnish Sámi Pedar Jalvi, who both came as runner ups with their debuts in 1915.

With this presentation, I have sought to show that *King Ahab - or Falk and Jenny* is a novel about injustice and forgiveness that seeks to mediate an overly broad social chasm, where the subtext concerns ethnic differences. It is written by an author who gave the production a somewhat divergent perspective, but was working his way towards an identity theme. This coincides with the author's own identity construction through his work on the naming of his own author-persona.

In 1904, the same year as a constitutional commission for Sámi rights concluded that all reindeer-herding nomads lost all of their privileges and assimilation was launched as an overarching instrument, Matti Aikio released a novel in which the hero was secretly a Sámi in disguise. At the same time Aikio declared himself a Sámi. But only partly: the author is keeping up appearances by keeping his Norwegian middle name Isachsen (which actually most frequently was used by Norwegian Jews). At the same time the hero of this novel Falk Fløiberg is – like his author – a master at social climbing. This mastery is only feasible as long as a possible Sámi ethnicity is kept hidden from the persons in the text. And as long as the text's topography is a southern exposure, this can be maintained. Things will get worse in his next novel, where ethnicity becomes the main topic. Still, social ascendance is a possibility, but it immediately becomes more difficult as soon as the hero moves around *In Reindeer Hide.*

IOANNIS SCHEFFER
Argentoratensis
LAPPONIA
Cum Privileg: Reg.Majest.svecia
Francofurti & Lipsia
Impensis Christiani Wolffii Bibl
A: 1674

— So Ahab came into his house sullen and vexed because of the word which Naboth the Jezreelite had spoken to him; for he said, "I will not give you the inheritance of my fathers." And he lay down on his bed and turned away his face and ate no food.

I

The river came from the mountains to the north and emptied into the bottom of the fjord on a level with its cliff-filled, curving shore on the west side. The small, rapid waves hurriedly lapped the cliffs, yapping like puppies, then emptied into the fjord and tapered into a large, long, impressive tongue quietly smoothing out at the sides in keeping with the somnolent sea surface. The river current down deep merged with the heavy main water, curved off to the left and went into a bay behind a large, flat sandbank on the east side of the river mouth. An angry strip of waves showed how the currents chafed against each other.

Right up from the bay a path led through a scanty woods up to Captain Steen's estate above the highway. This led over the river bridge and farther along the cliff-strewn shore to a copper mill owned by the captain's cousin, Fritz Hall.

Halfway between the bridge and the mill structures ended a strip of woods that went along the riverbank on the east side and was owned by Captain Steen. It adjoined a barren rocky mountain that with old maiden prudishness prohibited the frivolous organic materials from soiling their numerous progeny onto itself. But for fifteen years it had to tolerate humans martyring and persecuting its finest nerves, the copper ores, that seemed to want to allure the desirous eyes right into its guts.

Farther to the west and north, bare mountains looked bluish; but toward the east, wooded ridges rose in leisurely steps.

It is about midnight in the latter half of August. A disguised man has lingered for a quarter of an hour down in a thicket on the east side of the river and close to the bridge, and in agitated indecision said Yes and No to whether he should dare cross the bridge or not. Just think, if someone spotted him! Captain Peter Steen in disguise! What would that mean? What a scandal that would be! And scandals he has always avoided like the plague.

And in any case, maybe someone might guess it's him? Make spiteful, tacit ditties. "There are fifteen years of old hatred that have now finally flared up."

At this moment he could hardly believe himself that he was really on his way to set fire to the copper mill. — He took rapid strides into the woods to sneak home. But then he stopped suddenly. He had heard hearty peals of laughter from the festively illuminated doctor's estate up on a hill above the highway – halfway between the river bridge and his own estate, and which he could barely make out between the tree trunks. The laughter came from his own tutor, law student Falk Fløiberg. They were celebrating the district physician's birthday. But the day should also have been the occasion of a larger event. The two cousins were supposed to – it was the assumption – meet at this party and seal the reconciliation just like that in silence. The captain had actually decided to accompany his family, daughter Jenny, her fiancé Assistant Pastor Jakob Richter, tutor Fløiberg and the housekeeper, old Miss Magda Naadheim. But at the last moment he had excused himself, saying he was ill.

…

He listened. The lonely thoughts had frightened him; but the distant human voices dampened the feeling of fear. His courage rose anew. "I think I'm a coward!" He almost calmed down and managed a real smile, and it felt so soothing.

"Bah! It isn't, damn it, a crime I'm going to commit! Just a little business transaction, a – if I may say so – a fine diplomatic courtesy to get the chance to help Hall." He smiled ironically at his own dumb cowardice. "Of course, I've said it a thousand times to myself that he wouldn't be in need of money if the insurance settlement turned out to be too small. — The main point is that he will be forced to turn to me! Difficult situation, it might be said. — The creditors have been here. Maybe the fire would be welcome for Hall too."

And with these noble thoughts Captain Steen changed his mind completely, ran over the bridge at full speed and disappeared into the aforementioned strip of woods below the rocky mountain. He stopped a little while to catch his breath. His heart was pounding vehemently and his eyes became misty quite involuntarily. He began to regret having dared cross the bridge. How would he get back without being discovered? If he wanted to go back again, he would risk at any moment running into guests from the party. But on the other hand, it was not by chance he had chosen this night to carry out his project. It wouldn't be so easy for anyone to miss him at home when the family was at a party. Nor had the boys returned yet from their summer vacation trip. In other words, there could hardly be a better opportunity. …

At each step he instinctively took toward the mill buildings he asked himself whether he was really fully serious about setting fire to the mill. — He had come all the way to the fence that ran along the edge of the woods. From here he could again see the doctor's estate with all rooms lit and with windows open. The night air was calm and it was quiet. He could hear the music and the happy voices.

Good God, how strangely alien Captain Steen felt now! Not many minutes ago he was at home walking in his own rooms. And now he thought his own estate and woods and everything he could see in the moonlight dawning at this moment on the other side of the fjord bottom – all those people who were now at a party – everyone it seemed to him was so distant from him, and everything was so unfamiliar and new to him! His entire life which had grown together with the woods and the people here at the bottom of the fjord, now almost seemed to him like a dream. He felt like a baby bird that has fallen down from the nest in the tall tree. Never would he have believed that a person in such a short time could be estranged so far from himself and his own. This feeling captured him so strongly that he deliberately had to think of it. If he were now to come home, then he would almost have to take Falk by the hand to greet him – as one who has been gone a long time.

His narrowed, light gray, small eyes rested plaintively on the doctor's estate where he stood and leaned against the fence. His neck had sunk deeply down between his broad shoulders, which also always seemed to be its goal. His narrow lips hung down feebly; otherwise, he usually pressed them together, so his mouth looked like a cut from a knife, which appeared all the more when his moustache was clipped short, and the line from the root of his nose to the point of his chin was almost straight.

"I am unhappy!" he sighed. He had become sentimental in his quiet observations. He saw himself as an injured, persecuted and despised man. They all had it in for him! There was no honor and sincere sympathy to be found from anyone. Wasn't it perhaps out of pure evil that his cousin fifteen years ago had rejected his offer to become a partner? And Hall's considerate friendship with him while growing up and in the years of their youth – wonder whether that too had been calculated? — With the intention of presenting him, Peter Steen, as someone who needed to be protected by Hall – not economically; they both belonged to the village's richest and most dignified, but protected from oblivion and neglect.

And all the others were just the same too! Not a single one had a friendly thought for him.

...

But this bloody, sentimental dejection suddenly stiffened like plaster. What damn use was it to try to be upright! — Conscience! — The hell with his good name and reputation! Now he wanted, hell's bells, to let his hair down so that it would rattle in all the village's corners. If he was caught, then let it happen in the Lord's name! ...

His muscles tightened; his face veritably sweated hatred; he was bloodthirsty to wreak havoc, indifferent to what kind and whom it might cause to suffer. He was just about to snarl a gruesome oath, when all of a sudden he caught sight of a man coming sneaking toward him along the fence's outer side.

Indeed, hardly had the captain anytime previously felt so completely disillusioned himself from the slightest feeling of pride as now. He ducked down and close in to the fence. He blacked out when he heard dry twigs snap and rustle right close by. He capitulated entirely. — Then the fence creaked a little. The man crept cautiously over and stole, bent forward, over to the washer that lay closest, and disappeared behind a corner.

The captain didn't yet dare to move, but his heart trembled with grateful joy that he had averted what would have been worse than death.

…

Hans Braaten was a drunken worker with gypsy blood in his veins. A couple months ago he had turned up at the mill and gotten work. But now the mill owner had recently had to fire him because of much too much drunkenness. But then Braaten had gotten drunk worse than any time earlier. And remarkably enough, he always had something to drink. A couple times he had also had delirium. He was a human wreak who didn't give a hoot about most things in this world, which however was not an obstacle to him having a sort of sense of honor, in any case, according to his own notions – and of course vengefulness too. It was more anger at the bloody injustice inflicted upon him with his discharge, than the sorrow at having lost his daily bread, which a couple days ago had brought his mouth to boil over with violent threats against Hall, something he himself had later forgotten. But Hall had recorded it in his diary which out of old youthful custom he constantly had with him.

…

The captain lay still and held his breath. The man again came into view at the corner of one end of the washer, took a few steps back and forth and looked around the corners. Then he struck a match against his trousers, lit a plane shaving, quickly and carefully stuck it through a crack in the wall – and ran off. …

When Steen saw the blue blaze it was as if invisible forces put claws in him and threw him towards the woods. The air whistled around his ears. His lungs were filled by cold breezes, and tingling blood streams shot through his arteries. Like a wild deer he went at increased speed over stock and stone through the dark, gentle woods – without stumbling once. Ran, ran as if hundreds of voracious devils were at his heels. When he had gotten level with the bridge, he sank down and spit blood.

So movingly odd was this absurdly chance stroke of luck for him, that he – out of a sheer need to be thankful – at this moment was almost capable of believing in God, and it was he who had intervened in his enigmatic providence.

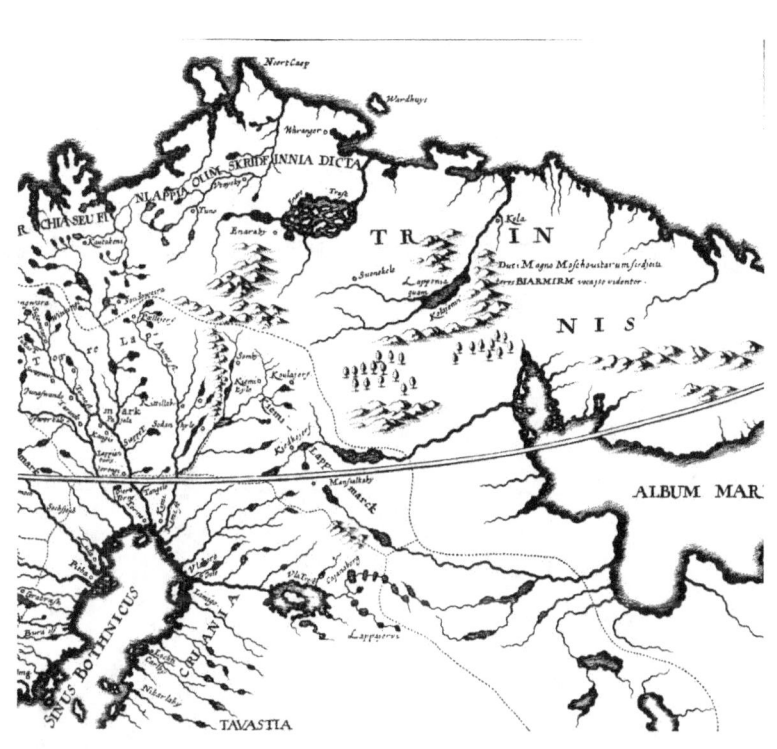

II

Contrary to usual practice, this time the guests showed up very early for the party at the district doctor's. With a bloodhound's sense people had gotten wind of the cousins moving toward reconciliation. And in order to gape at this reconciliation scene the guests this time had accordingly waived their stylish dignity of coming as late as possible; there was otherwise a regular footrace carried on when they were invited to the "Pastor's" or the "Doctor's" or the "Mill Owner's" – and earlier on to the "Captain's." The last one, in any case as far as he was concerned, had long ago withdrawn from society – or more correctly: people had over the years one by one distanced themselves from him in all silence. His wife had also been dead for many years.

If Per Stubberud and Anders Langgard met during the morning, then after a long conversation Per could ask quite by chance whether Anders was going to the Pastor's that evening. But Anders turned the chewing tobacco in his mouth slowly and answered with the most indifferent mien: "Yeah-ah – I don't know. — It might hap–pen. I'm invited. Yeah-ah. — I'll see whether I have time."

But these parties at the Pastor's, Doctor's, Mill Owner's – and previously at the Captain's – were in reality the year's red-letter days for people here at the bottom of the fjord. They already far in advance had an idea about when one of the big days was nearing. The days with regard to the calendar in status were Michaelmas and Midsummer Day.

Some were sure to be invited and looked forward to the day with a mixture of self-important calm and happy expectancy. But for those who were not confident they were right, this period of Advent was simply frightful. Even if one could be so fortunately situated as Jens Skvættebakken who had everlastingly renounced belonging to the hoity-toity and who nevertheless was a respected and revered man in leading circles. But this balancing on the border! Mrs. Langgard's despair once went so far that on a sleepless night she had to pray to Our Lord that the Pastor must not forget them. Nevertheless, the day came that time without an invitation. The Langgards put down their work entirely and sat and counted the hours; it's still not too late. One can hope to the last. And longing, anxious eyes peer out through the window. — The day came to an end; but no invitation had come there. Miss Langgard became a recluse to weep. And she who had lately begun to show herself off so well! She was even popular last time at the Mill Owner's. And now she had gotten her best gown ready – in hidden hope of being invited. Mrs. Langgard at first sat mute for a long time; but finally she opened her mouth with a sarcastic remark that the neighbor had been such a bootlicker to buy her way to the Pastor's party with a fattened calf. No, that the Langgards would certainly not do! No, never in the world would they! And Langgard himself sat and thought inwardly to what extent he henceforth should greet the pastor when he met him on the road. The blow felt so much harder that the Langgards had still not recovered from the grief that their first attempt to give a party for the circles had cost them. The party had cost them fourteen days of work. They had held a dress rehearsal. The mistress of the house had her role as hostess down pat; smiled and was well-mannered and friendly with a vengeance. But, ach! They had not taken the world's malice into consideration. The obviously fine ladies had in all secrecy organized a strike. No one came other than Jens Skvættebakken and Fløiberg who sat the entire evening like two Bedouins at a fertile, rich oasis in the desert. They ate, in truth, like two heroes, and – it's a shame to say – they drank more like sots than is proper for modest guests.

...

As said: contrary to usual practice, this time the guests had arrived at the party very early. And now people were excitedly waiting for the captain's arrival. The guests were festive and expectant, as if they were going to witness an exciting drama. They almost forgot to speak; only here and there could a secretive whisper be heard. This unpleasant silence had a depressing effect on Hall. He understood the reason for it. He had nothing to reproach himself for with regard to the origin of the painful relationship between himself and his cousin; but all the same, he was beginning to regret having come here to play a drama for the many gaping eyes, although at the same time he desired a reconciliation with all his heart.

Finally, those on watch by the windows caught sight of the captain's family coming walking up the hill, first Jenny and her fiancé Assistant Pastor Richter and old Miss Naadheim in tow, and a way behind them law student Fløiberg together with a crofter who was also going the same direction. Besides, it wasn't just chance that Fløiberg wasn't walking with the others. When they had walked past him and the crofter below the hill, Jenny had repeatedly looked back and tried to catch his eye; but he had with brutal indifference refrained from looking up and seemed to enjoy himself splendidly at the crofter's riotous talk. Then Jenny had become silent. This quiet scene Richter noticed. And although otherwise he was never narrow-minded and spiteful in speaking about others, not once in speaking about Fløiberg, this time though he became bewildered enough to make a couple remarks about Fløiberg's most recent scandals – really to start a conversation. But then Jenny turned to him, looked him in the eyes and said: "Jakob! Cause a scandal! Cause a scandal, I say!" — Her lips quivered. They walked silently up the hill.

The guests were to a high degree disappointed that they didn't see anything of the captain. Like people who have bought tickets at a high price – and then are gypped out of the actual performance. But Hall felt relieved.

Miss Naadheim entered with the usual sign in her face: "Here I am!," immediately began to parcel out her friendliness and had – as it's called in court reports – a friendly word and a friendly nod to one and all, an interesting question to someone or other, followed by an "Is that so!," accompanied by a coquettish, amazed expression on her face, when her eyebrows were drawn all the way up to the middle of her forehead and the "s" in "so" played affectionately between her teeth. After lifelong practice she had succeeded in getting her thin, uncovered eyes used to squinting, God knows why! Still she sat down with a young man in a morning coat who was always very busy being cultured. It didn't last long before she got into her old topic. "For my part I can hardly believe," she said, "that it is really the case as people maintain that young men preferably fall in love with older women."

"Miss Naadheim should be the last to be in doubt about that," replied a charming, fat lady. "You surely have a very rich personal experience in this respect."

Miss Naadheim was at a loss and almost blushed, tossed her head back and laughed, so her shiny, white teeth added luster to her mouth. She wet her lips with her tongue, stepped seductively on the young man's foot and pushed her arm into his. In short: she was like a brook trout singing and dancing with titillating joy – just thinks, but doesn't know.

Only the joy wouldn't last long. Her mortal enemy, Fløiberg, who this evening seemed to be in an especially brutal frame of mind, came and joined the conversation. He drew himself up into a stiff, solemn speaking position. "Well – it is Miss Naadheim's old topic that is on the program. May I be allowed to make my contribution to the elucidation of this question! First and foremost, it is a question of limiting the subject's outer extent, for which reason I will emphasize to begin with that it is ladies from 25-40 years of age, the young men can and often fall in love with. But it is only cats, lap dogs and little tots who fall in love with ladies past fifty – not to mention those over sixty.

He said this, because everyone knew that Miss Naadheim was over sixty. The callous disdain in his glance somewhat off to the side and the painful but at the same time brutal smile that now played around his mouth as he ruthlessly parted with one bit of malice after the other, was a spontaneous outburst of the inner crisis that he was just in the middle of. He had to scold.

This morning Jenny had broken the silence that had reigned between herself and him since this spring when he came back from Kristiania. And she had done it in a bold tone and with words that were full of indifference. And with the pious silence, which until now had been like a discreetly whispering brass between the two of them; with it the thoughts' clandestine conversation was interrupted. It was as if the air no longer could bear the quiet, soundless words between them. And that harmed him exceedingly. Jenny saw this. At first she felt somehow satisfied with this. Finally, she had become impatient with him keeping strictly away from her. She had in vain tried to approach him amicably. …

Fløiberg had to scold. People were aware of his thoughtlessness, when he wasn't in the right humor. Therefore, an unpleasant silence spread around him. You almost did not dare to open your mouth; for he could break in with a boorish remark. He even stood there and enjoyed the effect of his presence, blew smoke rings up in the air and sipped his glass conspicuously too often. He looked impertinently rigidly at old Miss Naadheim who was on the verge of shedding tears and didn't know what was becoming of her.

Fløiberg himself knew better than anyone else that his behavior was imposing. And this tickled his almost abnormal vanity. He felt with delight how people's eyes – and above all Jenny's eyes – rested on him where he stood with his hands behind his back, his supple, lively legs placed a bit apart from each other and his head bent forward. The loose-fitting frock coat became him splendidly. He was on the whole well attired; but then he had used his entire year's salary for his wardrobe, and more than that: he always greeted the tailor very respectfully. His weakness was the steel grey eyes; they were too small, he thought. "Oh, God! The one who had had large eagle eyes – a large animal's look!" he could sometimes exclaim when he stood in front of the mirror, and did that almost constantly when he was alone. The hair on the top of his head was already somewhat thin. He had combed it down over the steep, straight forehead into two or three apparently carelessly arranged tips. His profile with the high, gently bending nose and the powerful chin he preferably showed off. People called him thus the man in profile. …

The unpleasant silence was broken when Mrs. Langgard, who as it happened wasn't present for the previous arrivals, stepped in and, well-bred and used to drawing rooms, walked over the floor to a group of gentlemen, nodded smiling to Richter and said: "Howdy, Mr. Pastor?"

Of course, the genteel ladies put their heads together and criticized her almost aloud. Just think, saying "Howdy!" Arm in arm they went into another room, and here it was unanimously decided that Mrs. Langgard should be boycotted at parties. They also took into their confidence the doctor's wife; but she protested very energetically and thought that Mrs. Langgard would soon be like the rest, and that "until further ado one ought to be well-mannered enough to tolerate her little foibles." This protest had the effect that the ladies humbled themselves to converse with Mrs. Langgard, and finally she was shown actual courtesy. The ladies had discovered a new way of being well-bred. Mrs. Langgard sat there the entire evening so radiantly pleased and elated from all the good food and wine and all the effusive amiability on the part of the men.

*   *

*

After the meal the guests separated into the different rooms and formed larger and smaller groups, while the host went around offering cigars. An atmosphere had finally come to the party; the tobacco smoke and the drone of voices filled the air, and the wooden, loose-jointed characters now found it easy to move from one place to the other and sit down without any further hesitation and balancing. Mrs. Langgard laughed with all of her round, rotund body, thumped the old pastor's wife on the shoulder and asked whether Jenson – the "morning coat" – wasn't "tolerably entertaining." "Oh, may the devil notice me! She laughed. And with her chubby hands she slapped her unreasonably enormous fat thighs, so they plopped with a smack, while tears of laughter one by one trickled down over the round peaks of her cheeks. The "morning coat" you see was paying court to her daughter and was witty. "Haven't you heard, Miss Langgard, that the *ansjos* – or anchovy as it's pronounced – lays its eggs in the can?" —

Fløiberg in the beginning had pushed the acting so far that even his intimate friend, the doctor, who was much too familiar with his weaknesses, looked very indignant. Now he had started to become mellow and penitent., though without being despondent. Well, he had snarled, he thought. All things considered, Jenny's calm language after the scene today had been warmer than ever before. He could celebrate a victory in silent joy. A mild ecstasy had settled like a veil of elegant colors over his soul, desirous for life but always hungry, and gently blew his irascible nerves to rest. He walked out and down to the garden and sat on a bench.

Jenny's eyes had followed all his movements. Even the finest nuances in his mien, in his words, were like captions in his mental life that she knew by heart; her own, inner feelings were an echo of them.

She knew that he was now sitting down in the garden. Therefore, she took up a position in one of the windows in such a way that he could see her.

And Fløiberg understood the motivation for her standing there. Now, when the first violent, terrible swings had abated, now it was as if the old, quiet longing again had awakened, strengthened in its renewal, fermented by the mild ecstasy, dragged and lured up by the wistful and absent-minded expression in Jenny's face at the window; an expression he himself had engraved, and the consciousness of this gave him the beautiful peace of self-reconciliation.

All the old memories from four years ago when he came to Captain Steen for the first time as a tutor, now stood large as life before him. Jenny was then, although only sixteen, already a nubile woman. And in his happy moments he always had to move her back to that time in his thoughts. It was as if he then came closer to her. Good God, how her body could play affectionately and supply. She swam in the relaxed flood of the great and glorious longing for life, sang and laughed and danced and listened with open nostrils, jumped and smiled, blushed and suddenly turned serious, almost unpleasantly serious, grew sad, and then the dark blue color in her large, fervent warm eyes could become almost unfathomably deep.

It would take a colder, far more sophisticated nature than Fløiberg not to be captivated, helplessly captivated by this fully mature sixteen-year-old woman. He had just come from the examination bench. The half year he studied for the university entrance exam had been unpleasant and bitter, a life in hunger and petty deception.

His childhood home had been between the mountains high up in Gudbrandsdal where his father moreover was a guide for tourists in the summer and a hunter in the winter. However, his father's greatest mystery in this world had been: who did his son look like? His mother was dead, immediately after he was born. Shortly before his death his father got a promise from his old friend, the mountain Sámi, *Várre-Vuovde Nilas* (Nils from the mountain woods). That he would rear his son, and so it happened. A fortuitous turn of events brought him at age seventeen to Kristiania.

...

The sight of and being with Jenny was the first aroma of culture that hit him and filled his senses. Her voice, the soulful expression of joy and of sorrow, the beautiful, illusory clothing, the richness of the environment – all of that which until now had been a fairy-tale castle for him, took his breath away. And Jenny loved him with all of a passionate woman's first love. Could he wish for a more beautiful fairy kingdom?

...

He peered into it with a child's piety. Therefore, he didn't dare knock on the door, but with his senses confused went to sea the year after, got all the way to Africa, was gone a year, came back to Kristiania and stayed there the following year. With bewildered senses and worn out he had returned here last year – although he knew that Jenny was engaged and perhaps exactly for that reason. He then felt more confident, and here he had to come.

...

Much had changed from that time and until now when he sat in the garden. Now he was in a position to admit to himself that Jenny wasn't actually what one would call a beauty; in a sense his vision and thought had become more critical. He found pleasure in this, his superiority. The somewhat strained features around her mouth and the wings of her nose made one think it was a little difficult for the skin to stretch over the nasal bone; but at the same time they seemed to be absorbed by sensual passion.

Her bust came every bit to her advantage since she never wore a corset in any form, just a snug bodice – preferably without pleats; for she dimly perceived the bewitching power that lay in her bust – as in the deep, hospitably appearing hips on her long legs. She was a woman in full.

He got up. At the garden gate he met Jenny. They both wanted to say something; they both wanted to stop; but they didn't stop and said nothing.

Fløiberg went in. A frisky and seductive joy streamed out of his face and all his movements. The guests saw it. In a jiffy he had seduced them. His sins were forgotten. He sat down for a while with the old pastor's wife who with all her rigid propriety was unable to resist this big child who bathed in the unreserved joy of life, risen right up from the moment's pure and blissful heart. … "Isn't it funny, Mrs. Størum, to get together on a beautiful evening like this? People at a party, nicely dressed – look for example at my neat suit! – People are enjoying good food and wine. Everyone is in a holiday mood. Young people are fascinated by each other's ardor, and the elders are swept along. I have seen old folks who at a party have almost felt youth's swinging depth beneath their feet." – He burst into a hearty laughter and whispered into her ear: "Look! – Look, the handsome old pastor is casting such stolen, loving glances at you! – You, Ma'am, must have been a beautiful, young girl, such a slender, dignified female figure who hovers between the trees in the garden. Isn't that so? One of those who can get young men to jump up on the heights or hide between the trees in order to spy through binoculars for hours."

A gracious, blushing smile lay over the venerable pastor's wife's face. "I don't know what one can do with you, Fløiberg. It is impossible to get angry at you, even if one never had as much reason to do so."

…

Herewith, Fløiberg had done away with the strongest, final wall of rigid correctness. Now he allowed his joy to pour forth in all its unbridled boisterousness which as always was and inevitably free of the vulgar. The spontaneity even put its charm on rude remarks that otherwise would have been intolerable at a party with proper moral conduct.

Song and laughter and music and dance and play filled and teemed in the air far into the night … Several times Jenny and Fløiberg were on the verge of speaking to each other; but they didn't do so. They tried to smile to each other but couldn't. Only the eyes spoke. …

"... In admiration for all women that God gave the capacity for great love, we empty our beakers," Fløiberg ended his speech for the women.

"Fire! – Fire at the mill!" shouted someone by the window. The filled glasses that people were just raising to their mouths, clanked crashing over the floor: everyone ran to the windows, looked out again – over and past each other, scratched and elbowed each other down as if there were a fire beneath themselves.

But before anyone else had yet had time to become really frightened, mill owner Hall was already at top speed down the hill and over to the shore; he seized the back stave of a boat by the forelock that went out onto the sea with such speed that he had hardly gotten in himself. He rowed with superhuman strength. Suddenly the flames licked high up in the air, so the forest ridges and mountain wall and the houses and the sea shone really devilishly. Hall got up; but just then the boat swerved into the path the current followed. It made an abrupt turn; Hall lost his balance, fell down into the sea and sank; an oar popped up a moment later — He was missed only when the rest of the party came to the mill. ...

Fløiberg could not help noticing how people were busy becoming frightened and grieved by the disastrous fire. It was as if they consciously enjoyed this feeling of now being worried and distressed on behalf of others. As too an animal joy concealed itself that now something had happened which could shake the sluggish, apathetic nerves. But they forgot the most important role of fright – committing a real thoughtless act. At an orderly pace they all left together – except Mrs. Hall who in helpless desperation was running back and forth, not knowing what she should do – and Hall who on a wild impulse wanted to row over instead of driving or riding the short way around the bay. ...

The sea of flame flowed over the mill buildings. It flashed and crackled and boomed as in a battle. When the fire reached the oil and petroleum stores the flames shot with thrilling might high up toward the sky and twisted in majestically beautiful lines that teased huge snakes on bright embers. The smoke filled the calm air and lay above like a powerful, black thundercloud. The mountain wall was showy with the fire's reflection, and the sea surface shone gray like the transparent skin of a corpse.

Mrs. Hall ran around with a heart-rending shriek. "Fritz! — Oh, find him! Find him, for God's sake! Find him!" People had to hold her forcibly from going into the flaming buildings. She thought that Hall had been burnt inside. Finally, the fear overwhelmed her. Half demented and fainting she was again driven back to the doctor's estate.

...

The fire – this greatest characteristic of hell – had in a few hours transformed to dust and ashes what human hands had collected and put together over many years.

*　　*

*

Captain Steen lay in the woods – huddled up like an animal scared witless. He heard the tramping of snarling, galloping horses and screams and shouts that hurried right past him. ... Where should he go? Would people miss him? Bewilderment seized him totally. ... But then suddenly he gets an impulse: he sticks his entire disguise in under a wind fallen tree. He could run over to the mill in just shorts and pants and shoes of course. Then people can think that he just jumped out of bed. And in his joy at this scintillating idea he even tosses his stockings away. — "He didn't even have time to put stockings on, people will say. And thereby he ran off to the mill.

III

They both belonged to the village's most distinguished, had a govern-ess together and were in the same class, although Peter Steen was three years older than Fritz Hall. When they later entered school in the city, Fritz was favored and preferred by the teachers and classmates, and the girls competed to play and talk with him. Fritz learned early to un-derstand what feelings this had to arouse in his cousin, and with his tact he got the latter to be his equal in games and friendly company. Peter could sometimes sit a long time in quiet admiration of his cousin and mull over what sort of a strange power dwelt in the little fellow. But the fact that his own popularity should be so fully dependent on his cousin, at the same time formed a small suffocating lump in his little heart. Fritz too understood this, and he could therefore sometimes pretend he was really competing with Peter and was jealous.

Life kept them together over the years. They had attained a tru-ly glittering dexterity in playing their roles with each other. The whole thing looked like a friendship, such a deceptively honest friendship that they perhaps themselves presumed it to be a friendship too.

Only a single time did Steen have the feeling that he really had moved closer to his cousin. And that was when he for the first time in his new cadet uniform promenaded down Karl Johan's Street. Then the young girls had looked more at him than at Hall. A whiff of power from himself – and not from his cousin! How it felt lovely! He had a charitable feeling that at this moment he didn't hate his cousin; he could well have embraced him. When he came home he stood in front of the mirror, and with a sincere heart he thanked God he had the uniform.

Hall had begun to study scientific subjects. But there came a period in his life when quite a few of his type can slide down into – debauchery. He was a person with large and strong swings which his gentle temperament at the same time could not master. His unfailing self-control in comparison with his cousin – it had grown up as a distinct desire.

When Steen saw how Hall's life began to develop, it was as if he grew a couple of feet in his own eyes – and partly in others' too. It was simply astonishing to see how his self-consciousness suddenly grew. There were even those who thought he was more gifted than Hall. "Steen has a profound temperament," they said. This he got to hear himself too. It echoed in him for a long time; he listened and listened. — "Profound temperament?" wasn't that so? And then he had to say it aloud again and again to himself. And the words echoed for a long time in his mind, and he listened as a child listens to an exciting fairytale. "Profound temperament" … He could almost be tempted to feel sorry for his cousin.
…
Lieutenant Steen had taken over the estate after his father and had gotten married right afterwards. The same summer Hall arrived – after many years' absence – at the home village, and "had a dozen bums with him," the lieutenant said. In his student days he had during a short visit home found copper ore in the mountain on the west side of the fjord bottom. Now he started to blast the mountain, and people almost weren't able to sleep at night. Steen often said to the neighbors – as he smiled ironically – "Hall certainly must be very busy destroying his money. He couldn't destroy it quick enough abroad. It goes quicker when he shoots it up in the air." —

The following year the copper mill was already in full swing. Then Lieutenant Steen came to Hall one afternoon, and offered himself as a partner.

Hall walked home with gloomy thoughts. "He lay down in his bed and turned his face to the wall and didn't want to eat."

Now for the first time he dared admit to himself openly, how deeply he actually hated his cousin. It blazed in the old, soot-filled fireplace.

During the hours he now lay awake at night, all of the gall bladders that were ready to explode opened. He was ready to suffocate from this yellow sickness that lay so impenetrably impervious over his soul; this monstrous phlegm that seemed to want to suffocate him. There were nothing but humiliations all the way from his earliest childhood to now. He saw his life sullied by everything he had had to grin and bear. In vain he was seeking an honorable, self-won victory. "Hall is an insidious snake!" the lieutenant said as he beat the wall. He was sweating from insults and wrath. He regretted bitterly that he hadn't long, long ago broken up with his cousin. Oh God, that he himself hadn't been the first one to come out with insults! Now he was even supposed to bear the humiliation himself that he had tried to force his way into Hall's business. Oh no, oh no, if only he himself had been the insulter! Not even that honor would he get.

*   *

*

The years went by. Rarely, by accident, the cousins could meet on the road. They both tipped their hats, but didn't exchange a word.

At one time, Hall for a long while had believed that his cousin was not willing to reconcile. One afternoon they came driving toward each other on the road. — "Are you going to the bank's board meeting in the city tomorrow?" asked Hall when he stopped his horse. But Steen had one of his most hateful moments then. He too stopped his horse, but didn't say a word; he just stared hard at Hall, stared impudently derisively at him. He stared and smiled absolutely, brazenly, such as he was wont to do when his bile was at its most bitter. Bewildered and with an almost dumb smile Hall repeated the question without getting an answer. He rode off, dumbfounded and ashamed. The captain – Steen had now become captain – turned and followed him with his eyes for a long time and smiled. He enjoyed his triumph with sincere contentment. For once a genuine victory. He didn't remember his first victory when the little girls on Karl Johan's Street had looked more at his new cadet uniform than at Hall. — He laughed. "Don't you think he looked shamefaced?" he said to his farm hand who was driving him. He simply forgot it, and he, he who was so afraid of the simple! — the simple in disclosing his intimate affairs of the heart to the farm hand. — The hand was jubilant that the master of the household let him in on such piquant stories. He spit so far out of contempt for Hall as if going for a record. And with a fervently candid enthusiasm, he made derogatory remarks about Hall with his rural terms of abuse.

The hand got a few days off. He began to dominate everyone in the servants' quarters and boasted about his intimacy with the master of the household. It was "me and the cap'n" incessantly.

…

The captain's great strength consisted of silence, the hard staring look and the long, brazen but irritatingly dumb smile. His wife died from his five-year silence that began when Hall – three years after Steen had gotten married – led his young, charming wife to the mill. Then the captain immediately began to compare. From that day on he almost didn't say a word to his wife. When she tried to say something to him, she met only a long, hateful jackass smile and a long, hard staring look from his small, squinting eyes. And this frightful silence rested like a nightmare over the whole house. He literally silenced her to death.

Also his circle of acquaintances became smaller year by year. He walked around his large estate, lonesome and abandoned, feared by his subordinates and despised by others. In his most bitter hours he could sometimes wish that he had an enemy that really hated him – but not even such did he have.

IV

For many years Captain Peter Steen had stared at the copper mill until his eyes were half blind and bloodshot, which grew steadily and became busier over on the other side of the fjord. It was as if he thought his own woods and fields at the same time were fading and dying – from that curse that Hall had naturally conjured up over him. His eyes were closed to all the magnificent, fat plants that teemed over his own fields, to all the sap-filled woods that incubated millions of lives in the large roots, tall trunks and proudly rocking, full branches, earth so rich and luxuriantly generous against the sucking pores like a mighty mother's breast against the suckling child, closed to all the mysterious treasures and paintings and engravings that are kept in "the museum," a special room in the very old, but still well preserved building. Yes, even the captain's uniform had long since lost its power of attraction. He just listened to how the yellow glistening copper ore during booms and bangs loosened far inside the bare, shiny rocky mountain and sailed down the rope tracks in the air and down to the washer. Wasn't it like gold falling down onto Hall directly from heaven! — Hall's unabashed, open face also seemed steadily to be turned upward, out of gratitude toward the good Lord. And all the friendly, trusting eyes he met everywhere! While Steen's own face steadily became more and more distorted and darkly squinting from grief – from the curse that Hall had conjured up over him. The silence around and at the captain's estate had in recent years laid a ghostly gleam over it. People walked past with a certain wary feeling, as they hastily cast a glance through the dense, high bushes around the garden that lay down by the road, sort of to get a glimpse of the dragon in a virgin forest. When the sun went down behind the rocky mountain on the west side of the fjord, it looked as if darkness threw itself with greed over the captain's estate.

V

But one beautiful day people began to hear a beguiling, hearty laughter and boisterous speech in there in "the dragon's nest," to use the village's witty tailor's words. There were those who claimed they had heard the captain himself laugh. The captain had gotten a tutor. The children had until now had a governess.

Jenny, the oldest, had just taken the middle school exam; but this coming winter she was going to study French and literature with Fløiberg to prepare for a stay at a girl's boarding school in Germany.

The quick-witted, congenial, cross-eyed Adolf, or Doff, as he was called, was going into second middle. Doff seemed comical, especially when he cried. Even a stupidity from him – wise people can sometimes be very dumb – had the effect of a congenial joke. He also stammered a little. He could become so strongly impressed by his own reports that he involuntarily made faces when he couldn't find a convincing expression – like the smith who couldn't crack the nut with the devil between his teeth. Ingolf, who was going into first middle was somewhat bashful. His tricks always backfired before he was done performing them, and then he became shamefaced. And yet he was, strangely enough, just as dogged with his attempts to win approbation.

When the farm hand drove the new tutor into the courtyard, the captain came out and laughed toward him. The boys lay on their stomachs up in a clothes closet on the second floor and inspected their future tormentor through a little window. "Look, how stiff he is, boy!" remarked Doff.

In the garden room two ladies sat with needlework. "Miss Naadheim, my daughter Jenny; Student Fløiberg," the captain introduced. This immediately broached the subject of school affairs and let Fløiberg clearly understand that he, Fløiberg, had come into the house not as some nobleman, but quite simply as a tutor. — "Has Jenny studied French previously?" Fløiberg directed the question to Jenny herself. But no sooner had he cast a glance at this full-blooded, mature, sixteen-year-old girl than he suddenly realized that he had made a faux pas by saying Jenny instead of Miss Steen. And at the same moment, another difficulty arose too that he couldn't solve. Should he address her with a formal or informal "you." You Jenny, you Miss Steen – he was completely at sea. But another thought occurred to him as well, a vision of quiet hours with Jenny. He was entangled entirely in this seductively gentle, gilded veil of future visions that welled forth so thrillingly. The captain was at the moment on an errand in his office. Jenny observed with astonishment Fløiberg's sudden, bashful silence, while Miss Naadheim racked her brain as to what she should say to get the conversation started. — But Fløiberg awakened from his dreams fervent and fiery; he talked ceaselessly and brought both the captain and the others into the most pleasant humor. The boys heaved a sigh of relief after he had said hello to them and spoken with them most amiably. They had to go into the servants' quarters to tell the farm personnel what "a very pleasant" teacher they had gotten. And such an illustrious man!

Right after Steen had decided among the applicants to employ Fløiberg, they had come across a little notice in a little Kristiania newspaper. It was about his life up in the mountains north of Gudbrandsdal. "No, my God! He must be interesting," Jenny had said. "Just think, he is coming here."

*   *

*

Already the same afternoon Fløiberg got the boys to accompany him up to the copper mines. This was very much against the captain's will; but the boys were irresistibly enthusiastic to get an excursion. Besides it was of course the tutor's first day. Although afterwards the captain, when they had already taken off, regretted that he hadn't said a definite no. He was given to being regretful, the captain.

… When Doff during the evening lay half asleep in his bed, he thought he was seeing noisy animals with avaricious eyes and foaming, blood-red mouths come down from the mountains. The Rondane mountains, Fløiberg had said, were so high that when you stood on the highest peak, you could almost thump the vault of heaven and stick your finger into a star hole. Doff of course thought that it had to be a joke, but anyway … The clouds lay underneath like a leaden, steaming sea, which, when there was thunder and lightning, boiled like a flaming sea of fire. Above, the birds sailed and shrieked with fear over the ghastly sight. Rondane is shrouded in a hollow spinal column of blue, crystal clear, powdered ice, wherein one can see the flashes of lightning split colors as in a prism. It may happen that Rondane is inundated by the sea of fire … Doff bit into the bedspread.

But there could also be high-born silence up there, with distant, muffled music from running water. In spring when the glaciers shot blue green ice tracks down over the scree slopes, and ether-chasing mountain tops to the east and west and north light up like white swans bathing in the morning sun's shimmering rays. The waterfall boom in the rocky crevices farther down slowly climbs up like a ceaseless, sometimes stronger, sometimes weaker growl and the snore of trolls far inside the mountain's interior. The reindeer grappled and struck their loosened antlers from one another. The blood lies like a net of scarlet thread out over the sunny pale snow and dark green ice. But in the midst of the still life suddenly come the wolves and spread fear and confusion over the entire mountain, so that it is a horror. The reindeer move in wild flight in all directions to avoid their sworn enemies, and the Sámi and the little, ragged Finn dogs leap up and fly after the wolves like little wads of feathers in a heavy storm. The hollers and yells and barking and wolf howling resound like a ghastly chorus around the wild mountains … Doff fell asleep.

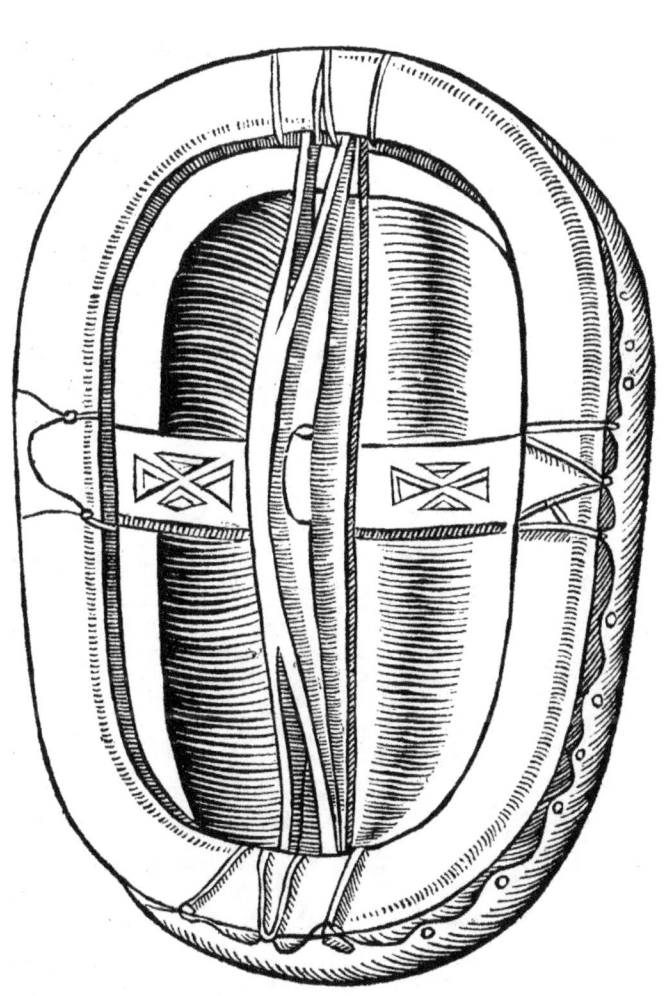

VI

The devil had unexpectedly gotten hold of the captain's finger and taken him completely by surprise. Fløiberg played nobleman all the same. The captain swore and cursed in his core that he was immediately going to put a stop to this so that Fløiberg thus owned up to setting aside all considerations of master and servant. Well, well, damnation, there was going to be a stop to this! He would show that he wouldn't let himself be hoodwinked by a common tutor. For otherwise the fellow could hit on behaving like a swain to Jenny too. The captain had worked himself up red-hot as he walked and made small talk with himself in the office. He had had the wool pulled over his eyes. Fløiberg's advantage when the captain chose him among many other applicants was supposed to consist of – judging from his own written information – his being an innocent from the countryside, a modest, at most somewhat greedy dwarf birch from the mountain, and to boot past the horniest age; he was already twenty-three. But the captain had a pig in a poke. God help him! If the fellow doesn't turn out to be in possession of qualities and an external appearance that can be very dangerous for such an amenable and naive nature as Jenny. He behaves with a disconcertingly self-important flexibility, although he hardly ever in his life has set foot in a salon, hardly even an educated shoemaker family's parlor. But the captain should have known how Fløiberg really was!

VII

Fløiberg's college friend, Karl Eide, sometimes used to say to his friends, to be sure with a little hint of a sarcastic, ironic smile, that he, Fløiberg, was a born gentleman. "It's really only among well-bred people you feel at home," he turned to Fløiberg himself as he intensified his smile into a bitingly ironic seriousness that made him go out of his mind. Fløiberg for sure tried to make his remarks into a joke and wash out the satire by means of a smile or laughter; but he couldn't conceal that he felt targeted: his lips and the creases up under his eyes quivered feebly and insipidly and bore an all too clear stamp of embarrassment, an embarrassment that Eide couldn't use enough during the ensuing pause. In Eide's vicinity he always felt as if on embers. The cutting remarks lay in the air as an electric charge, and he knew that Eide seldom refrained from pressing the button. For it was so with Fløiberg that he had a sleep-walker's instinctive skill in going to places with pitfalls all around; but a little puff could push him down into the abyss. As for example last fall when on summer vacation he stayed with Eide, whose father was a pastor somewhere in Western Norway. The first couple days Eide had been forbearing. But one afternoon he fell to the temptation. He and Fløiberg were going to go on a fishing trip. When they walked into the guestroom where Karl's sister and another woman, by chance as it happens, were sitting writing letters, Fløiberg said: "Excuse me, ladies, we're going to have a quick wash." Eide cast the most mischievously serious and surprised glance at him. "Have a quick wash? — Where did you learn that expression?" Fløiberg turned blood-red in his face. Maybe he had said some indecent filth? No surer was he in the use of the Norwegian language, which not too many years ago he besides had had to begin learning anew. — "Yes, it's true for that matter," Eide said after a short pause (on such occasions he always used a short, but effective pause); "but I didn't think you were into such cultivated expressions." Fløiberg wasn't haughty enough to accept it as a harmless joke or to be certain that the ladies of course couldn't hear a witty satire in Karl's amazement. "What is it you are going to have or wash, then? — to use your own expression," asked Eide. The question paralyzed Fløiberg, singed his nerves like a red hot poker. He of course didn't have any traveling clothes with him, for the good reason that he didn't have any. The women pretended they hadn't noticed his embarrassment and hurried out. Which didn't improve matters for Fløiberg who surely understood their thoughts all too clearly. This act of mercy by the two gracious women settled as a heavy weight on his already previously so heavy humiliation. — The following three weeks that he spent with Eide became a single, ghastly torture for him. It was worst during the meals. He couldn't participate in the conversation. Eide could sometimes direct a couple words at him; but Fløiberg misunderstood him as a rule and could then give a harebrained reply or also say a short, sharp "What?" — "Hello, man – axe handle," mumbled Eide, half annoyed and smiling with his mostly merciless, funny characteristic around the mouth, while Fløiberg cast a glance at him with an expression that at the same time burned with wrath ready to burst and a doggishly pitiable plea for pity.

"Today the farm hand is going to drive down to the city. It might be convenient for you since the steamship is going east this evening – yes, isn't it so that you've been considering traveling one of these days?" You see, it had already gone a couple days past the agreed upon time Fløiberg was to stay with Eide. And he wouldn't have hesitated to travel if only he had money. He had lain many and long nights and again and again experienced the coming scene with horror, when he was going to ask Eide for travel money. He had imagined his face in the most different expressions: friendly, mildly understanding, amazed, annoyed, at a loss, sincerely courteous, but the fundamental tone in the expression, sarcastic irony, he couldn't blot out. — It was, all the same, Eide who broached the travel money question, and that even – to Fløiberg's joy and surprise – in a liberal, fine form. To be sure, he couldn't refrain from giving him a little sarcastic remark shortly before the departure. "It was mean of this fellow that he didn't send you the thirty crowns he owes you. Just think, leaving you in need of money in that way!" Eide had known very well the entire time that it was a little lie about the thirty crowns that Fløiberg had spoken about already on the first days; but usually he was never in a hurry to drag Fløiberg's many small white lies and other frailties into the light. He took them out in fitting portions. And Fløiberg devoured them with an embarrassed smile, and often – to his own terror – with hardened shamelessness; for that which tore and continued to tear the roots of his heart later, was that he himself daily was witness to how his feeling of shame lessened and lessened and lessened – right out appallingly much! He had become sensitive to petty criticisms that a manly superiority ought to strike against, and tough where a strong feeling of honor would denounce them abruptly.

But there was neither anyone who could inflate his vanity more than Eide. "If it is as I have heard hinted that there is French blood in your veins, then you are certainly a direct descendant of Napoleon, albeit one degenerate to the highest degree. Yes, degenerate to the highest degree – naturally, on a tourist trip of course one can't expect anything better, so much the less, since it in all likelihood happened on a spree." Now, when the talk was about his little crumb of resemblance to Napoleon – this cutting, ironic resemblance, now Fløiberg could tolerate everything and anything at all, yes, if only he resembled him even a crumb more, then he should gladly give half of his life, renounce all his better qualities, be the greatest coward on earth! Eide could so extremely willingly be allowed to sneer and rake him over the coals in front of the entire world, only at the same time he wanted to make people aware that he, Fløiberg, was an apparition and a real, but to the highest degree degenerate descendant of Napoleon. Yes, Eide could possibly say that he was a scion of a cut off, half rotten slice of a nail on one of Napoleon's descendants big toes. — Every time an agreeable soul gave a little hint of his likeness to Napoleon, it was as if a powerful wave lifted him up from the depths and handed him over to powerful eagle wings which carried him dizzyingly high up into the blue sky with a view to all the earth's corners. His steel gray eyes then could impossibly be as small as he himself believed. But, ach! The looking glass maintained the lamentable fact. "God, the one who had a big animal eye, with a blue color as deep as the South's sky!" If only he could cut, hew away the shameful Mongolian features that stuck out like weeds at the expense of the noble, romantic lines. Wonder whether it would hurt, and whether it would grow back somewhat handsome? That part there ought to go, and that too – and then add a little there. But then one would also, may the devil dance, get to see Napoleon!

No, there was something so deceptively appealing about Karl Eide's flattery. He reviled him at the same time. A justly sober division of light and shadow! Fløiberg could be touched by gratitude to Eide.

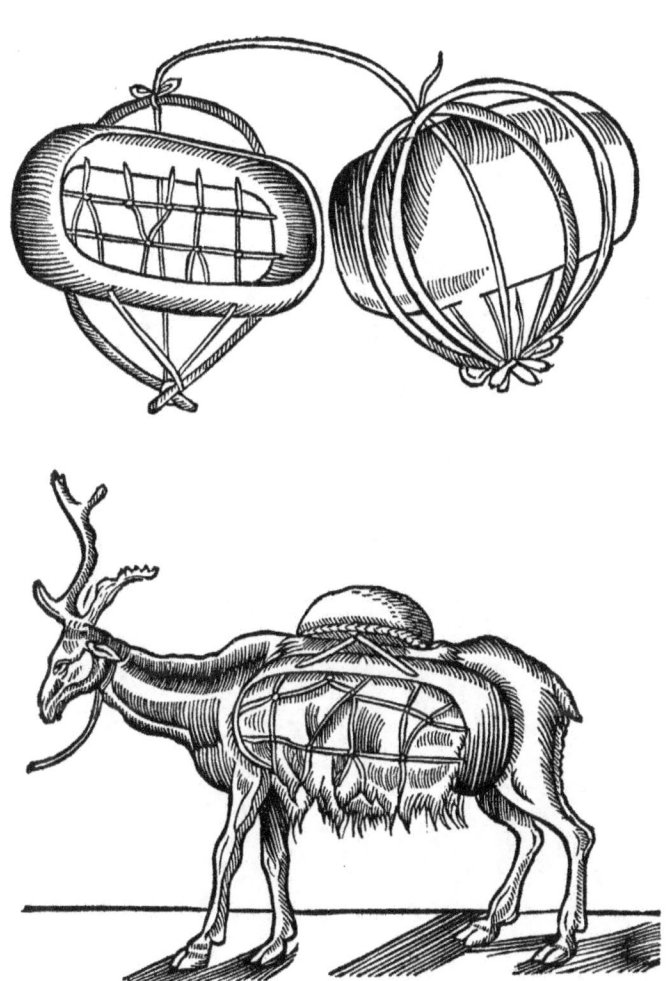

VIII

His threat to put a stop to Fløiberg's complacent and much too irritatingly confident behavior the captain had not implemented. And when at long last he had dug down through so many layers to discover the sensitive and weak – the cowardly with Fløiberg, it was already a bit too late. Sheltered by the pleasant conceit that Fløiberg now for over a month had been able to bask in, his resistance had grown to a degree surprising to him. The captain's attempts to establish a haughty, durable expression, slipped away without making Fløiberg confused. The good, and what also promised to be, lasting upper hand gave Fløiberg a tickling feeling of manliness, a rare feeling for him, whom every puppy could put to flight, bring into confusion by just showing its teeth. In his unrestrained joy at this strange, saving stuff in himself he could occasionally be tempted to err, to go beyond the line that in the captain's eyes formed the border for the proper. Like a young woman who for the first time feels a living being move in herself.

At the same time there had cropped up in the captain, almost unbeknownst to him, a strong sympathy for Fløiberg, this cheerful soul in the good fortune of the moment with his charmingly boisterous and orotund laughter. No, he couldn't get around to causing the ill will that would lower Fløiberg a few notches and in the future create a proper distance between master of the house and tutor. He didn't have the means to extinguish the spark of life lust that had been kindled in himself. Alien and hostile he at first had stood against it like a captive who in hardened desperation has spent many years in a dark prison and, cursing, turns away from the light that suddenly is brought in to him. But it held onto him anyway, drew him to itself with an irresistible power. He constantly had to have Fløiberg with him. If the latter went out during the evening or was together with others, he became jealous. Sometimes he tried to make fun of himself – to steel himself. He couldn't openly admit to himself that the fellow had become indispensable to him. — Other times he felt apprehensive, especially when he saw that Fløiberg was in a mixed brutal and unrestrained mood.

This happened the first time one evening before Christmas; they were sitting and drinking highballs.

"Don't you think, Captain, that it is grand to be master over so much life? Own it, so to speak. This tangled life of countless worms and maggots – they of course belong to you, live off your land – and cats and mice, hares and birds that sit at your table daily too – not to mention all the magnificent cows and horses, sheep and bunnies, chickens and geese that live like princes and princesses with appanage. And all the luxuriant trees and plants that gorge in luxury! If I was lord over so much life, I would feel like a little god."

The captain cleared his throat. But on the contrary a wild contumacy seemed to bob up in Fløiberg.

"In blind, godlike fury," Fløiberg continued, "I would chop down an entire colony of trees and shout: "My hand, the master's hand, has met you! But not a word! — Shut up, I say." — And you louts of worms, I'll trample you to death, if you don't extend your bellies down to the ground."

He spoke with a brutal abandonment. The captain became bewildered, anxious — Was Fløiberg drunk?

"But I would also," Fløiberg went on, "swap roles. I would go to other ages, depending on how I was so inclined, fall on my knees before my subjects, worship them, kiss the dust the worms eat, make sacrifice to rats and bunnies and weeds. I would beseech them for grace, flatter them, swear solemnly and sacredly that such rats and bunnies as I have, hell's bells, not seen on all of God's green earth – although I have just been in a fairy-tale castle. The sparrows that come here to the garden, I would wait on with strawberries and roast turkeys on silver platters and champagne in polished beakers."

The captain got up, quiet and with a mien that clearly said that this he didn't find amusing; it was an unpardonable irresponsibility of a tutor to speak in this manner in front of a student, and besides a student who was a young, innocent girl. Such, Fløiberg had not allowed himself before.

...

It's marvelous what a young woman with newly blossomed senses can smell. A bud ready to burst, whose magnificent hiding place sunshine and the damp, rich earth opens one beautiful day. But the slightest wind gust, every drop of raw, plump rain that pours over it without first being cleaned and warmed and enriched in the soil and the fine roots of hair and cells – the thinnest stream of cold can leave a mark in the ether pure colors, frighten the chaste petal that bends together and watches over the precious, holy treasure, the fruits which longingly in their shelter await the fine threads as a first greeting, a first kiss from the pollen that hovers above, and whose presence they suspect. As also every touch of tickling warmth; the weakest puff of the sun's delicate golden rays can cause the flower to unfold in prayer into an open embrace; More! More!

...

Already the way in which Fløiberg filled his glass – a little noisily, hasty and impatient, but at the same time with an indifferent mien, had convinced Jenny that this evening there was something exceptional about him. All of a sudden it occurred to her what the reason was, a discovery that got her excited, made her dizzy. So she didn't need to be disappointed after all.

...

During French hour from six to seven in the afternoon the captain usually sat in his office and now and then let the door opening into the corner room in the left wing stand ajar. There was a tacit, three-sided understanding in that; neither Jenny nor Fløiberg could dare to close it once it was open – it stood, was supposed to be open.

The hour was always the day's solemn occasion for Fløiberg – and for Jenny. Both began to wait for it to come, longed for it already in the afternoon.

When Jenny stuck out her foot under the table, Fløiberg knew very well that it was to touch his foot; but he didn't have the courage to stick his out. When Fløiberg stuck his hand over the table and let it lie there, Jenny knew very well that it was to graze her hand. Every day and every night she lay awake in her bed, she had made up her mind to let her hand slip over to his during the next lesson – just think, if he would grasp it, hold it firmly, press it warmly, with tears in her eyes! But when it came down to it, she couldn't

…

Today, when she wasn't able, or more correctly, pretended she couldn't find the line Fløiberg had begun to translate for her, he had pointed to it in her book – just as she had figured, she had of course beforehand pulled her hand back; but in the moment's emotional uplift from the first sensation of his fine, white hand she had involuntarily and directly against her will jerked her hand to the side. It was as if an electric spark struck her. But at the same moment something cold too went down Fløiberg's back. They burst and burnt, all the full, explosive illusions, broken and gobbled up by the voracious disappointment. But he controlled himself. Not an expression, not a word gave away what had just happened to him. Not now. Jenny's conscious and clear attempt to repeat the experiment failed. He pointed to be sure: but just as consciously this time he avoided touching her hand. And yet he was just as friendly when the hour had ended, albeit a bit stressed which Jenny seemed to notice. Maybe, Jenny thought, he hadn't understood at all, hadn't devoted a thought to what she for over a month had gone and thought about, tortured herself with. Had she completely misunderstood him? She felt disappointed, she too. But she, unlike he, couldn't hide her feelings. She sank down with them. And Fløiberg read the pain in her face, heard it in her voice. But at the moment he couldn't convince himself that it really was Jenny's intention to make amends for it when she anew couldn't find the line.

…

And when at the end of the hour he went up to his room, he threw himself down on the sofa, but jumped up again. He had a bad conscience. Terrible to make erotic approaches to his own student! Just think, if Jenny absolutely refuses to study with him. He has caused a scandal, there's no doubt about that. And so laughable! How could a homeless beggar like him pay court to Captain and Proprietor Peter Steen's daughter! To a sixteen-year-old girl who was even his own pupil! His own pupil! — Nonsense! He said. He laughed. "My hand has by chance for a hundredth of a second been in contact with her hand. And for that reason I regard myself as a morally dilapidated subject!" He laughed so that he shook. "And then she is not at all my pupil. That I give her an hour's private instruction in French during the day cannot then oblige me to put on Saint Anthony's cape of smoked, dried skin. She's a grown woman …"

…

But Jenny had certainly jerked her hand to the side, it suddenly occurred to him. His heart knotted up and something suffocatingly heavy settled on his chest. —

"Yes, I wanted it," Fløiberg said. He had become milder and more jocose in his voice and in his expression. — "I wanted to get a sculptor to make symbolic statuaries of all my animals and trees and plants and servants. Ola the farm hand would stand above the door of the servants' quarters as the keeper of organized life like the rooster he is when he crows people up in the morning and sees to it that everything takes its regular and assured course. The milkmaid and the ox should be sculpted in marble and placed each on their own side of the entrance to the cow barn. A large potato should stand on a high pedestal in the middle of the field, with a roof over."

The captain couldn't refrain from breaking into a smile; but so as not to seem like a weather vane, he turned away and walked to the window. He contemplated the garden with an attentiveness as if it were the first time he had looked at it. A thought that suddenly appeared occupied him strongly: I should rather be afraid of than wishing it would go poorly with Fritz. I have it, could have it good, as I have it like this. — It was the first time he tried to take comfort in this manner; but it was something new anyway, something warmer about the thought this time.

Jenny saw that Fløiberg's pipe had gone out, and that he wanted to light it again. She got a box of matches for him. He looked up. She smiled a little and blushed. A little awkward and, her hands shaking a little, she struck a match and handed it to him; but when he was about to take it, she didn't let go of it right away. He looked up again; her eyes became misty, not from tears, but from the stirring sigh and life's abundance that at certain moments swells up in a young body. He pressed her hand, warmly and quickly: his eyes too became misty, not from tears, but …

IX

The resounding laughter that passersby again and again had heard throughout the autumn from "the dragon's nest," had gradually abated over the course of the winter.

Fløiberg wasn't laughing any more.

Only in the boys' school hours could he still occasionally let himself go. The school room was a large dance hall on the second floor above the garden room, still with a row of chairs and sofas along the walls, but which hadn't been used since "the curse" came over the house. When the boys knew their things satisfactorily, he could sometimes get into a good mood. It had almost become a fixed fare that as a weekly reward for diligence he put on a show. He made faces with a phenomenal dexterity, as if his face were made of rubber, mimicked people of the village – not even the captain went free – and he always hit the characteristically ludicrous in them. Drew caricatures of them. Jumped up on the table and held raving speeches. Told how up at Rondane he had stood and looked into the heaven through a star hole. He had seen little fat angels with jovial, little horns. The boys squirmed with laughter. They lay on the floor and laughed with tears in their eyes until their stomachs hurt.

...

From that evening she handed him the match, and until after Christmas there wasn't a day without Jenny and Fløiberg exchanging long handshakes during school hours.

One Sunday afternoon they sat alone in the garden room, while the captain took a nap after dinner. They were sitting next to each other at a little table. Fløiberg brushed her hair, and she brushed him on the chin. They almost had to stretch their hands, they couldn't move closer to each other. — "Let me see the ring," he said. "No." — "Yes, I want to." He grabbed her hand. There arose a little struggle. She came to sit on his lap, and her cheek touched his. Then the struggle stopped right away. She felt with her one arm how his heart was beating, strongly and rapidly. There was a long and calm listening to the feverishly warm music of beating hearts. Further they didn't get; but that far they had never gotten before either.

Then they heard voices out in the vestibule. They jumped up, and in walked the assistant pastor Richter newly arrived in the village, a young, blond, clean shaven man. The somewhat too short nose and the slightly crooked, light eyes gave his open, engaging face a certain humorous, half comical character. It was Miss Naadheim who had opened the front door for him. God, how she had been gorgeous!

… Excuse me, Miss Steen, dare I be so free as to ask whether you have had coffee. — Not? Good! Then you will, let us hope, treat me to a lovely cup of coffee. — As an apologetic factor for my boldness I can besides allege that your most honored father, the captain, has invited me to drop in here for afternoon coffee today." He rubbed his round, well manicured hands and made gymnastic gestures to warm himself.

…

A month or so had passed. Jenny and Fløiberg weren't exchanging handshakes any longer. No longer.

And the laughter had subsided.

Jenny and Fløiberg and Richter could often meet at parties or home at the captain's.

Richter then usually always had a lengthy, pleasant conversation with her, while she in vain tried to catch Fløiberg's eye. And then she could suddenly break off the conversation and go over to Fløiberg, but he answered curt and turned away. She could hear in his voice and the short words a silent shriek from a bleeding heart.

…

One afternoon in June Fløiberg walked into the office and said to the captain: "I'm going to travel with the 'Roland' that's in the harbor." — "But I hope that you come here again when you have traveled enough," said the captain.

An hour later the three-master steered out of the fjord …

Jenny comes home from an afternoon visit with a girlfriend of hers and meets Miss Naadheim at the garden gate. "There sails the Roland," says Jenny.

"Yes," answers Miss Naadheim. "And Fløiberg is on board."

"Has he left?"

"Yes, he has left."

"That isn't true! Oh, say that it isn't true!" She breathed out a sad scream, and her chest tied up.

She ran down to the shore and waved and shouted agonizingly painful: "Fløiberg! – Fløiberg! It's me, it's Jenny!" At a wild speed she ran farther along the shore and tried to shout; but her voice drowned in tears. The 'Roland' disappeared behind a point; only the large mast could still be seen for a while. Then she suddenly stopped. It was as if the hard truth only now stood clear to her. She bit her lips bloody, tore up her bodice and fell down: she thought, she certainly had to die.

X

The year after Fløiberg came back from his long sea journey that had gotten all the way to the Congo states.

Right after – one of the first days in September – he met Richter up in Bogstad Street in Kristiania.

Yes, she was doing just fine; had often spoken about Fløiberg and wondered where he could be. "You ought to take a trip there. For example, at Christmas. You will certainly be welcome. Jenny was in Germany last winter. But now she is certainly at home for the time being."

Richter spoke candidly and directly as he had always been in the habit of doing. To be sure, he knew about the earlier relationship with Jenny and Fløiberg. But good grief, young people have permission to love each other without it therefore having to become something suspicious for life. This he had taken comfort in, every time Jenny had begun to speak about Fløiberg, every time she after the long pauses sighed heavily and said a disconnected word, which he understood was always about Fløiberg. But now they had drifted apart. Jenny had become an adult and wiser in the ways of life, had had her eyes opened to values of a solid worldly life. And Richter himself belonged to a cultured pastoral family.

But on the other hand Richter had taken a real interest in Fløiberg with his somewhat fantastic history behind himself. It would be enjoyable if something could become of him. He had also recommended him to his family and several of his acquaintances, in case Fløiberg needed advice in word and deed in one direction or other. But his fine discretion prevented him from saying it directly to Fløiberg; he only asked whether he didn't feel like becoming acquainted with his family in the city. "You who are such a lively young man and have traveled and experienced much, would be a dear and treasured friend of the family."

Richter's unfailing warm-heartedness disarmed Fløiberg who though was not able to avoid noticing the care whereby Richter chose his words when he spoke about Jenny.

Richter himself was only temporarily here in the city to familiarize himself with the home mission, which from his youth on he nourished great interest in. He mentioned in all modesty that he had brought about a continuation school out there in the village, had taken over the leadership of the youth society and so on. — Intended to remain there? Yes, for the present in any case.

All this Fløiberg interpreted in his own way.

The old pastor would presumably in a couple of years take leave. And now Richter had already begun to smooth a good, solid path to the position. And wouldn't the circumstances under the captain's leadership steer Jenny's steps to the parish?

...

Fløiberg excused himself; he had to move on. But he hadn't gotten around the street corner before he stopped, had to stop, in fright. It pounded in his temples, whistled in his ears. His brain case seemed to want to burst, and his heart beat violent, rapid beats. He tried to think, but couldn't. Not even the hate of Richter could form into a thought, a ghastly thought that was capable of clearing the air.

...

After a wild, brutal, stormy life over eight days he awoke one morning. He had used up the last cent of his money, and was now sick and heavy in his head. But what surprised him to a high degree was that he nevertheless was in an almost giddy mood. That was a riddle to him. He didn't have a trace of the vale of tears that the day after is usually so inordinately rich in – not to mention the need to dress in sackcloth and ashes as an eight-day bender usually evokes. — He walked out.

It felt so pleasingly delightful to be able to inhale all the warm *joie de vivre* that now came tumbling in over him – from where, he couldn't explain! It came from all directions. The yellow leaves the wind loosened from the trees' branches seemed to sail into death in grateful joy at having been allowed to live a beautiful summer and breathe along in life. Wasn't it so that all the people he met were also walking in festive delight today? And the air was dizzyingly high and clear.

He had come all the way out onto the fortress point. He sat down and took up some papers he had in his picket. — An anonymous letter from Jenny! — It was just a few words, good, warm, simple words. The letter was addressed to the Students' Association. He had found it there yesterday evening.

Yes, now he understood from where this overwhelming, fertile joy emanated.

"Naturally Jenny is fond of me. This business with Richter has only been a fatal delusion of mine. — Now I want to work! Now I want to work!"

Again his chest was filled with overflowing joy. He had to hide from violence in order to thank – thank, well, whom should he thank!

"I don't know who you are, my God. And maybe you don't know either who I am. Nor can you perhaps hear what I'm saying, and know what I'm thinking. But in case I see a person who is looking for you, I will whisper in his ear that you are great. So great that it's no use praying to you or looking for you. In case people found you, and in case you heard people's prayers, you wouldn't be great. You are great in your blindness, in your cruelty, in your incomprehension. I thank you for letting me live."

He had his mind full of plans when he came home. The following days he spent writing a couple travel accounts from Africa that he was so fortunate to get accepted by the city's best situated newspapers. And, in addition, one of the editors was so kind as to let him collect a fee in advance. Well, well! It was of course a good beginning. Later he could get a suitable job as well. The Eksamen Philosophicum he had to pass before Christmas; but then he also wanted to study some law on the side. He had some legal texts still in possession from his time as a tutor.

But there was one more thing he had to steal a little time for, a little botanical treatise that he had worked on during his long sea journey. He read and wrote with intense energy, day and night. The awakening vitality ran away with him; he almost couldn't hold back. Three large herbaria and different moss types and insects partly in alcohol bottles and partly pinned on steel wire in boxes lay spread out all over the room. The collection was his sanctuary that he could show to people whom he in advance had convinced himself would properly appreciate getting to see it.

...

Reindeer moss and heather and strong herbs that drink with roots in crumbling minerals, had been his teeming throng of childhood friends on the high mountain. A man of science who one summer was studying the high mountain flora up there had told him many wonderful things about plants and insects and taught him how he should preserve them, the same man, who later got him to travel to Kristiania and helped him up to the middle school exam, but who unfortunately died sometime after Fløiberg had begun to study for his university entrance exam. From the Sámi he had also heard many strange legends about animals and plants which got his boyhood fantasy in motion.

...

In the course of fourteen nights he had his botanical treatise ready. The trick was to get it accepted by a professional journal. And no one was after all more surprised that it could be printed than he himself.

"Look, look!" — He got going on a newspaper article. That too brought in a small fee. He was beside himself with joy. Read with almost superhuman strength.

...

"Sentimental value." He became absorbed in the chapter with voracity. Read it out loud again and again. Took long walks and thought about "sentimental value." He built an entire world view on this concept. It wasn't just jurisprudence that lay in it – no, it was all humanity's good fortune. He gathered all religious ideas into it. "Sentimental value should be concentrated in the material and the present moment," he said out loud finally to himself. He thought that he had solved the riddle of life's salvation.

And with that he hurried home to begin on his great philosophical treatise. "It will be my life's great work," he said as he gesticulated wildly and sat down at the desk. But he had to get up because of difficulty breathing. The thoughts were streaming way too violently into him. "The work can be of epoch-making significance for all of mankind. — I'm standing on the balcony in Paris and receive cheers from the jubilant crowd. 'Long live the god of the sunrise!' sounds over the world city. I become so moved that I cannot hold the tears back."

He stood in front of the mirror, almost had tears in his eyes and wasn't really in agreement with himself about which way of bowing was the most impressive.

…

Again he had written a huge pile. But at the same time he had fallen lamentably behind on the way to money. He hadn't eaten dinner in recent days; supper and breakfast he had at his proprietress.

At the same time, the illusions began to burst. "Oh, if only I could fib myself full for a few more days!"

…

For a couple weeks he went around waiting for a reply from the editor of a general periodical. Finally, he dared to visit him personally.

"Well, I have read some of your work, but unfortunately I can't use it. It manifests talent; but it is much too immature …"

Fløiberg went down the steps with a relieved heart. Just think, so friendly and straightforward this country's famous man was! The editor was more than right that the work didn't amount to much.

A newspaper article he could still write. But it wouldn't work when he had sat down. The words settled so heavily and clumsy on the paper, and the content would in no way let itself be conjured up.

He was also on the go around the city looking for a job. But it was as if he couldn't do it really seriously. He found it so obvious that everywhere he was rebuffed. "I'm not really able to do anything much for which people could use me."

He spent the days partly at the Students' Association and partly on Karl Johan's Street. Mornings he usually made an effort to accomplish something, such as for example to approach people who might possibly be willing to support him in word and deed. But he always postponed it. Soon he had gotten apathetic and indifferent, was plagued every night by insomnia and unpleasant visions. Sometimes during the nights he could be seized by rage and fear that life was forever slipping out of his hands. "For many years I have stormed in a mad rush after beauty and complete happiness. I have always headed for what is central in life's great celebration; but I have always gotten outside the periphery. I have daydreamed myself into a soulful woman's embrace and wrapped in soft silk; but in reality I have merely had to stand outside a modest woman's door. I have daydreamed myself into the temple of wisdom: but, good God, how little I know!"

And then in the morning he could wake up in terror. At that moment his sensory nerves again begin their stirring, wonderful game; during the transition from sleep he had the feeling that he had already spent many years in this helpless state – that he was now standing there like a salt pillar thirsting and longing for water from its own bitterness.

To throw the moment's despair out – to make a really strong effort up from the frightful depth he had to say out loud repeatedly that in any case no more than a few months had passed – thank God! He had to hear the convincing words sound in the air.

But the days continued to hurry past him in miserly silence. Things had come so far that he impenitently accepted help in the form of loans of a few crowns from his friends; and Karl Eide was in any case the one he most confidently could turn to when money was scarce. And with the same brazenness he watched how his sense of honor day by day dwindled. But the fact that he could tolerate this could sometimes arouse fear in him. "If only I could run, run far away from myself!"

XI

Down through Rosenkrantz Street and down past the house roofs along Karl Johan's Street comes a stinging north wind one afternoon in January, swirls up cold, heavy street dust, flutters in the women's skirts that cling tightly around their starboard legs, knocks the top hat off one gentleman or other who in distraction walks right into the sewer grate – shrieks and plays wild howls of joy on the telephone lines that at the same time quiver from the city's gossip and serious business voices.

A well nourished, fur-clad gentleman is standing outside the corner of "Grand Hotel" and with the air of a connoisseur watching the various shapes of the starboard legs. Every time he sees that the wind is about to lift up a skirt, he makes an involuntary, strenuous movement upward with his one shoulder, as if to help the wind in its exertion as friendly people who are fond of children usually are attentive to the children's awkward efforts to lift little brother up onto a chair.

Fløiberg had stopped nearby. He wanted to try to stand at rest a while. But at the next moment he drifted inevitably on. He had to walk, walk, walk – although his back and his legs hurt, and his mouth was full of dust and dry froth that thirst and fatigue sucked out of his throat. His socks were dirty and sweaty and were clammy on his feet that had gotten sore and tender from the desperate, nervous pace up and down the city streets. But he had to walk. He had turned up his overcoat collar: the dirty flap he carried in his pocket. He tried to straighten his back; but it hurt, and then he let it hang forward as it best turned out.

He steered into the Students' Association and threw himself down on a sofa. He had imposed on himself most strictly to lie down for half an hour. "Take it easy, boy! Someone could come and invite you to lunch – Well, well, I can of course tell him that I'm thirsty and must have half a beer to begin with."

But hardly had he sat down before he jumped up again. You see he had remembered Harald Grimstad, the fur-clad gentleman outside "Grand Hotel." It was the most straightforward thing in the world to ask him if he could borrow a five crown note.

Fløiberg ran down the street. Quite correct. Grimstad still stood there. But since the wind had not gotten a single skirt further up than mid calf – and even though he had stood here a whole hour – that had given his otherwise kindhearted face an annoyed and disappointed character that scared Fløiberg. He hurried on and was even afraid to be seen by Grimstad.

…

Breathless he stopped outside the post office. He had again hurried at a furious pace without knowing why and whereto. — A yellow note could be awaiting me at home. Who knows! People are good. Incalculably good. To be sure, the money is coming rather late, but – he – Fløiberg could at the moment not decide who he was – he hasn't known before how sincerely willingly I need them. And to everlastingly put an end to my misery he has sent two thousand crowns. Maybe three thousand. His sister – it could well be that he has a sister – has also been willing to contribute a thousand. Poor girl! I will hell's bells marry her – just for the sake of her goodness of heart! And God knows – maybe she is beautiful too. She is one of the few ideal characters in our depraved era, he said aloud to himself. He scratched his neck and couldn't understand what great and good she can probably have heard about him.

It is of course she who has stirred her brother – or father or uncle or whoever it is – to agree to such a generous action. By God, I'll marry her! And such modest people! Send three thousand anonymously. So as not to risk a disappointment I will in any case, I will insist that there be more than three thousand. One shouldn't imagine more than it is, either.

A postman came out with a bundle of yellow bills. "Excuse me, there wouldn't happen to be a registered letter for law student Falk Fløiberg, Briskeby Road 26, 4th floor?" "I don't have that street," the postman answered, and went on his way.

Fløiberg awoke from his lovely feverish intoxication. He could feel the clammy, dirty socks on his feet. So very hungry he actually wasn't. Yet – it would be delightful to get a solid portion of hot food now. But most magnificent would be if he could wash up, scrub himself clean from all the dirty sweat. And then get delightfully clean clothes on himself! – Well, well, like that. He sauntered resigned up Karl Johan's Street again.

He stopped by the university clock. It was a half minute over six. A half minute. Naturally he had no use for minutes, much less for the halves; but he involuntarily noticed that the clock was a half minute past six. What if the university clock stopped? Perhaps it will stop in half a minute. He stood in suspense and waited to see whether it would really stop. And people don't know that it has stopped. They stand there and gape at their watches with dumb faces. Why don't they stamp on them? The pawnshop is open until seven. It would be a damn uproar if all of Karl Johan ran into the pawnshop with their watches. The chairman of the executive committee of the university with the university's clock under his arm. — "Name – where do you live, my good man," says the pawnbroker as he congenially looks over his glasses.

Fløiberg ran into the auditorium. He laughed at everything. The walls, the snow and the trees and the wind; everything was so funny. And the people walking stiff as twigs! — There are menfolk and womenfolk in this world. Menfolk are constituted this way and womenfolk that. The menfolk are wearing long, thick pants, and the womenfolk skirts that at the highest must not come further up than mid calf. But at night the people take their clothes off.

...

What if the university clock stopped all the same? What if all life stopped for a whole hour. Pause in absolute silence. All thought stops for an hour – where it is at the moment. The planets stop. All living cells stop. The dandy on the street stops just then; he has raised one foot up and bent forward to reach for his gloves that are just falling down. — Fløiberg stood and illustrated how the dandy would look. And lovers stop in the midst of their embrace. What a pain! To be in a violent thought for an entire hour. — Phew!

But just think, if Richter precisely at the moment of the stop kisses Jenny. And kisses her for a whole hour! No, that must not happen! Oh, God, that must not happen! Jenny is presumably at home now, and Richter – well, he is maybe out baptizing a dying infant. Well, well, the child can live an extra hour then, even if in silence. The water that Richter is about to sprinkle on its head, stops in midair during the fall.

…

And when the hour is over, it drips further down on the child's head: lovers can finally continue their embrace. The dandy can put his foot down and bend over for his gloves. True enough, his top hat falls into the mud: but he can brush it off on the sleeve of his topcoat. And the living cells swim on. The university clock and all the other clocks tick on. …

The one who had a thick gold watch to stamp on!

Fløiberg ambled on.

From Hægdehaug Road he swung into Oscar's Street, without really knowing why, and headed for a particular manor, also without knowing why. There's a woman singing and playing on the first floor. Does he recognize the voice? Oh, Ole, Ole, my own child." No, those weren't the words, just the melody. He walked closer to the window, and now he could clearly hear that she was singing with heartfelt, rising fervor:

> My glance hidden on you it rested,
> When most silent I sat and the blood hurried.
> My full heart did not calm down,
> It bade always that I embrace you
>
> In quiet appeals to you I longed,
> When storms wail, my boat will overturn
> You alone shine in the overturned boat's dark
> You alone smile, you, life itself!

He grabbed himself on the forehead, became warm and confused. What was that song which he seemed to know so well? And the voice. There was something in it that filled him with unease and awoke his slumbering senses. He walked around the corner. In one of the windows where the blinds were not rolled all the way down. He had to look in; he couldn't let it be. — His heart shot up so violently in him. He shook over his whole body and looked into the window like an astonished child that suddenly finds itself at the gate of the fairytale kingdom.

There sat Jenny at the piano, with her eyes turned almost directly to him. Oh, good God, those eyes! All of life's most beautiful warmth had flowed into them since he last saw them

She sat a long time silent – and then she burst into tears.

And Fløiberg cried like a little child where he stood outside, poverty-stricken and worn out, and froze and trembled in the cold north wind. If he could now jump in and take her in his arms, so they could both cry in each other's embrace. He ran back and forth in bewilderment – and he was lifted up by the gripping emotion that was now playing in all his nerves. — Jenny! He said a couple times. Jenny! — Jenny! — But the voice wouldn't, dared not go past his lips

…

He had simply instinctively walked here; he had also been here outside a couple times earlier in the autumn. Jenny's aunt you see lived in this manor. Only now did it dawn in his tired brain.

… It was nearly dark inside where she was; just the candles on the piano were lit.

Jenny gets up suddenly. The door opens, and a gentleman steps in – Richter! A slashing stitch went through Fløiberg's heart.

Richter wants to embrace her; but she shoves him away: "No – not this evening. I want to be alone this evening. You must excuse me …"

Richter turned pale. "Will this be a last clash between us?"

"No. You must not misunderstand me. But I want to be alone this evening."

Whether she was ill? – Yes – no, she wasn't. Pause … "I am still so very young – and then, and then …."

With a restrained motion Richter said farewell and left.

Fløiberg bent down at the garden fence so as not to be seen by Richter who walked right past him. Had Jenny allowed Richter to embrace her, he would now surely have grabbed him by the throat and choked him on the spot … without regard for the consequences.

Fløiberg too hurried away.

How should he understand Jenny and her conduct toward Richter? Was she singing with thoughts about him, about Fløiberg? — Wasn't the conversation between her and Richter a continuation of something that is already well on the way to – a little hesitation, then everything is finished. If only he knew what sort of a painful yearning was filling Jenny's chest – that brought tears to her eyes with such a melancholy sadness!

His eyes grew dim when he again suddenly began to think about his position and took a look at his clothes, noticed clamminess in all his nerves. — But as he hurries up one street and down the next, he suddenly gets a golden idea: the landlady can hand over just one set – and keep the remaining as a deposit until he can get some money. No, he hadn't thought of that before!

… When he got home at nine o'clock, he didn't even give himself time to eat, before he had taken the dirty, sweaty clothing off himself and scrubbed and washed himself over his entire body, almost in fury, so his skin became blood-red. He enjoyed with veritable piety the tickling soft, pure wool that settled so pleasantly comfortable over his body. And shining white starched material! And newly shaved!

"You may be sure it is nice to live after all," he said as he looked at himself in the mirror. "Falk Fløiberg has arisen from the dead," he shouted. "He shall live! He shall live! He shall live, until he dies!" he sang in boisterous passion. In the moment's elation he felt certain that Jenny wouldn't let him down. He suddenly remembered how he this summer, while standing on the jib boom with the mandolin in hand, suddenly sighted land and sang:

Open up! My soul wants in
To the fervor of your heart's rays,
My soul as wild as the forest's hind
And with longing as only love measures.

Come out to high summer rapture!
A song of animated waves
Blesses the silent, pleading sound
Of hearts that beat. — And light night follows.

…

The landlady, who came in with supper, was completely taken aback when she heard and saw him in this mood. She almost became bashful and modest. Lately she hadn't had the heart to ask him for money. She understood how he suffered. A month ago – at Christmas – he had even been gone three nights, when he didn't dare go home without money. But fortunately she had met him on the street and with a couple friendly words calmed him and got him to return home.

"Now I hope I will soon be on an even keel again," he said to her as he sat down at the table. "Oh, God bless you! — That was nice to hear! Yes, I congratulate you most sincerely. Don't bother about me, until you have taken care of the most essential of your own needs."

That awoke his own admiration that he had courage to refrain from saying that he now hoped for sure that in the next few days he would be able to get money for her."

… "You must not misunderstand me." He analyzed Jenny's words back and forth. How they stung him! — He tried to stand face to face with the apparent fact that tomorrow Jenny will receive Richter with open arms; but every glimpse of this thought hurled suffocating iron bands around his heart and pressed the blood up to his temples. He leapt up, had to quit in the middle of the meal, flew down the steps and out onto the street as if he were being pursued by evil visions. And suddenly he got an uncontrollable desire to experience something appalling that his white hot nerves could cool off in.

When he came out onto the street, he cut a deep sore in his hand. He had to see blood, red blood, that dripped down into the snow. If it was only spring up there on the mountain! With large scarlet patches of reindeer blood out over the glaciers.

… "Are you lying there weeping blood, esteemed friend?" — Fløiberg croaked. There stood Harald Grimstad with his jovial smile that always gave the impression of his two main characteristics, calm kindheartedness and refined sensuality.

"I cut myself on a nail over there in a gateway," Fløiberg said confused.

But a little after he took Grimstad by the buttonhole. "Can't you say something terribly bad, something that smells and reeks of hell, something – something that – that strikes marrow and bone and nails?"

The quick glance and the unpleasantly impassioned voice drove Grimstad back a couple of steps.

"Or do you want to take part in something terrible? — For you? And drink shots and be properly congenial? Many thanks, but I cannot this evening take part in anything so beautiful. — Good, if you want to treat me to something, then let us drive out to the suburbs. I know a man who every so often has to undertake a long trip here to the city just to bring a word of solace and a helping hand to the down-and-out here in the city. And do you know what? I mock the tramps because he is good to them. I wish that each of his mild, beautiful words would become a curse for the victims of misery, that every morsel of food he hands them will make their lips blue and thirsty, cause them to wince as during Prussic acid's poisonous force. Just because he – he is good to them!

The circumstance, Grimstad! — The circumstance. Now and then thousands of the most contemptible of the devil's great grandmothers dwell in such a circumstance. A circumstance can be so slimy, so heartless and so wretched that it unexpectedly comes and hits one in the face with the most poisonous vision, vision, that one would give his life to avoid seeing. It is this massive chain of snake-wise circumstances that robs and plunders us – enough of that. Do you remember that summer about three years ago. I could still have fun at that time. In the warm, sultry nights I splashed your fine, fat stomach with club soda. Or you stood a little way out on the balcony, while with the sprinkling can I dumped huge jets of water on you. I said crude things just to see your stomach laugh. It wriggled under your vest like a big flounder ..."

*   *

*

The humble restaurant way up Trondheim Road was filled by Fløiberg's powerful voice. He was blood-red in his face and spoke with deep passion. A bunch of drunk and halfdrunk guests had come flocking in from the various rooms and now stood listening. Fløiberg gesticulated wildly and swore that from this day on he would dedicate his life to the benefit of the proletariat, for his beloved martyrs. He had forgotten his original purpose: to deride ill-fated fellow beings in callous words. — "I am yours, I am like you; from this day on I am of the tramps. And among you I want to live." Here he was interrupted by storming applause. "The slattern" was moved to tears. "I shall organize a band of you all; you will have prickers everywhere like a hedgehog."

His eyes sparkled as he looked at his listeners. He already saw himself in spirit as a historic hero and martyr, drunk and moved as he was. He asked for beer constantly. And Grimstad paid. He understood that Fløiberg today was in that humor he had to rave his way out of.

...

When all the guests were chased out at closing time Grimstad wanted to drive him home. But Fløiberg got angry and swore that now he wanted to be with his tramp brothers. — "Home! I've never had a home. But now I have found myself a home I can say is mine." He had become sentimental and was weeping as he arm in arm ambled off with his "brothers." Grimstad followed a ways after them to see how things went. He wanted in any case to see that Fløiberg didn't end up lying outside. —

...

Richter and one of the home mission workers came at nine the next morning up to the "red field" to pay a visit to the various little wooden houses sitting randomly on hill slopes and earth mounds up there. "It looks like there are people in here too," Richter said as he stood and looked in through a broken window in a little, old, decrepit house. They walked in. Over in a corner lay four people snoring. Three of them were tattered and ragged, while the fourth one looked to be a relatively well dressed-man. This last one also seemed to be freezing the most. He lay on his stomach with overcoat inside out over his head. Besides he was wrapped in a horse blanket; it was evidently one who had taken care that he wouldn't freeze to death. The home mission man shook carefully the noble sons of Morpheus. A couple of them stretched their cold, stiff limbs and gaped as they emitted a little bellow, with a hoarse voice that pounded from thirst. "Oh, Let us for God's sake have some water!"

Richter went out for a pail of water. Also the two others woke up, and all four threw themselves greedily over the pail of water. But Richter moved back in fear when he saw who the well-dressed man was. He became embarrassed and didn't know what to do.

That lasted a while before Fløiberg came to his senses. It looked as if he at first was really not aware what was going on. He drank water and rested in between. And froze and shook and tried to breathe through his stopped up nostrils. The clean starched cloth from the previous evening had become dirty and soiled. His hair was dishevelled and his eyes wooden and red, his clothes dusty and soiled.

But when he then caught sight of Richter, it was as if the jarring dissonances from yesterday again began to echo at full strength. The intoxication still lingered in him. He got up and went over to Richter. "Now you can go and say that Fløiberg has become a tramp. It is your duty to say that. Tell everyone who knows me."

"No, I will absolutely not tell anyone. You can rest assured. This is just a little faux pas of yours. — I understand you well. You have an ardent temperament – I'm not going to reproach you in any manner. But now you must come with me into a hotel where you can wash up and take care of things. I'll buy you a new starched shirt. And afterwards we'll get a better breakfast …."

"Well, that you can by heaven get at Mother Larsen's over here in the street; then we can also, while we're at, it put away a little food," remarked another of the group.

Fløiberg looked stiffly at Richter. "The best service you can do me is not to try to help me any way whatsoever."

Richter was in despair. With a lump in his throat he asked and begged him to come along. "Believe me that not a word will leave my mouth about this little faux pas of yours." He probably didn't need to to assure him. Fløiberg knew well that Richter was a man one could rely on. But to the same degree he felt disarmed and mollified, to that same degree he forced out a brutality that struck Richter with fear – and even at this moment himself too. If only Richter though in one way or other had proven to be rejoicing in his down-and-out condition, said one or other word that smelled of a little debasing pity! Then of course he could have gotten a little foothold to stick his sharpest awl through.

"The slattern" gaped with long, blaring roars. "Now Grimstad shoulda been here and treated us to some beer."

"The slattern" said that they had been together with Grimstad, and that he had been a doggone generous and friendly chap. Richter knew a little about Grimstad. He got an idea and drove away.

"Will you be so kind as to take this hundred crowns and get your friend, Falk Fløiberg, placed in good care outside the city. But he mustn't get the slightest suspicion that the money is from me."

Yes, that was something that Grimstad would gladly be in on. He also himself wanted to contribute a similar amount.

*   *

*

When Richter the evening of the same day came to Jenny, a gentle, beautiful feeling shown from his face. His soul had been moved strongly. The softened repercussion from the shocking event brought color and fervor to his words. The evening twilight and the beautiful surroundings laid some of their strength on them. The handsome, charming people of his family to whom he had introduced Jenny little by little, provided them a base. And the new peace of mind that had come forth strongly today – its beginning he didn't dare admit – gave him the charm of superiority. — Jenny Steen and Pastor Richter had gotten engaged.

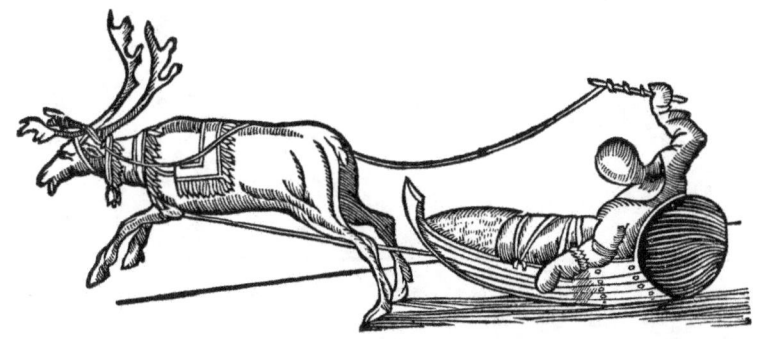

XII

Fløiberg had already been at the boarding house outside the city for eight days, when he heard about the engagement. One might have expected him to react violently. But that was not the case. He had had a showdown with himself, maybe too strictly, as one usually does after a violent bender. Nothing was left of him. He had sunk deeply and ruined for every last shred of his human worth. He had also wished he could be entirely liberated from his feelings for Jenny. And now this news about the engagement came as a release for him too. He breathed a sigh of relief. "Good God, why should I go and torture myself with such madness! — I, who am already such a bad person! — And am eating the bread of mercy!" And he hummed:

Cloud-covered sky; —
hoarfrost swarm
creeps so cold and wet and singing tired,
sleeps and dies, of the bodies full.

*   *

*

The following day he had to stay in bed. He had a fever, perhaps influenza.

It's evening. The lamp burns on the table. "Hush! — Quiet!" he says to the maid who comes in. He stares expectant and smiling into the air. With soundless steps Jenny and many other women come – he knows them all – down a ladder along the wall. "Close your eyes!" says Jenny. And Fløiberg closes his eyes. But through his eyelids he sees how the graceful, young women hover with light, rhythmic steps around the bed, fan his face with airy silk veils, incline and rock the room, which goes around with gorgeous, changing colors on the walls, while the young women hum:

> In play a tiger
> and wolf and girls
> and doves gentle
> all want to come
> to life's beaker,
> the deep sea,
> where little hunter
> – the little, frisky one
> with shell for float –
> the young blood in the cascade chases.

Jenny bends down to him and smiles so beautifully. Then Fløiberg cannot refrain from grasping for her; but as soon as he opens his eyes, Jenny and all the others disappear.

"Are you sleeping?" says the maid. — "No. Hush — still! I say. They want me to keep my eyes closed; for otherwise they won't come. — Now I have closed my eyes. Now you can come back. I want to prepare a bath in a sunfilled woman's breast." And they come back lined up in rows and rock his bed. "Isn't he a beautiful boy?" Jenny says to the others.

…

"Turn off the light!" he says to the maid.

He's on the verge of falling asleep when he suddenly hears people down on the street running back and forth and blowing into trumpets. The party, the year's big party has begun. The big riotous lodger. All his friends and acquaintances are gathered here. Yes, it is actually for him, they are partying. If only he didn't have such a cold, he would walk over to the window and greet them … But thieves have come into his room after all, dark, black clad people sneaking around on their toes. They near the bed with threatening gestures and shiny knives. But fortunately it occurs to Fløiberg that they are only his friends who want to have fun with him. — Hm, – they aren't even real people. They have just set up some optical instruments down on the street that conjure up these deceptive figures.

— No, he won't let himself be frightened. A black, shining axe is hanging above his neck on a thin thread …

And they're singing hymns and howling and speaking in comically solemn language down there on the street. "Up to Jerusalem! Up to the big city." "For the priest in Jerusalem I have nothing this time, but for the priest in Bethlehem I have four crowns," sing the girls who are sacrificing to the sect's priests who intone different Bible passages. — It is really priests from the time of the Old Testament. "A large, fat woman is a grand gift – yum-yum," says one of them to some devoutly listening women as he rubs his hands with relish. — It roars and storms in the room above where the musicians stand and blow into trumpets. They are playing "*Erlkönig*." The storm increases to a hurricane. The musicians can hardly stand on their legs, and the trumpet sounds swirl away with a steadily increasing speed and moving power.

What is it, these people, who stand around my bed, lead me to believe? — No, I am probably not sick. But I know why they want to lead me to believe that. They don't want me to come out and hear what a world famous man I have all of a sudden become. They don't think I am man enough to stand to hear it! — But if I have been man enough to become world famous, then by heaven I am also man enough to stand hearing it! The whole world is writing about me. The whole world trembles before me. But with some few words I have put the world on the risky edge. It depends on me, whether I will let it fall over onto the sensitive side, or whether I will spare it. It depends on me, me. The governments try to conspire to hinder people from paying homage to me. — Telegrams are arriving for me from Paris that I must go there. "Napoleon has returned," it sounds throughout France. Europe trembles with unrest.

…

Fløiberg goes daily to the city along a streetcar line. He goes with the entire apartment on the second floor.

There is intense excitement in the city. People want to hold a party for him. But the government has gotten orders from Russia to prevent all tributes to him. It is especially Russia. Fløiberg's mystical magic words are minted, they claim. They keep him captive in his apartment which is driven into a large hall in the city. Fløiberg understands that according to the tsar's request they want to send him to Russia. The emperor wants to try to persuade him to bring law and order back again. — "But I'm now doing what I consider right, anyway."

He goes with the whole apartment on the second floor across the Swedish plains. He is on the way to Russia. A lot of his friends are along so that he will not get bored. But they only come in one by one and still try to conceal it from him where they are carrying him.

It rushes along toward Russia's plains. Generals and diplomats appear at the stations amd make application to get an audience with him. And although he treats them like dogs, they must though grin and bear it. Oh, this lovely feeling of power! There are strong eagle wings that carry him high up beneath the blue sky. "I don't care how many millions this trip is going to cost. That's Russia's matter. But one doesn't need to imagine that for a few shabby millions I allow myself to be moved to do something other than what pleases me."

…

There is nothing that impresses him any longer. Not one expression discloses that he feels bewildered about this matter's new state. No, everything is so obvious to him. — The crowds flock together to catch a glimpse of him. His friends warn him against approaching the windows. There could be anarchists. "No," he says, "The anarchists only murder people – not me."

And the train goes at top speed into a forest of erect metal wires; but God knows where they come from: they disappear before Fløiberg's train like dew before the sun! …

XIII

The day after the fire at the copper mill, Braaten – the hellion – was arrested as under suspicion. He had, you see, also told others than Hall that he to be sure was going to defend his honor. Hall should not have fired him for nothing.

On the third day an interrogation was held. But Braaten denied with angry gestures. He claimed that several evenings in a row he had seen a mysterious looking man sneaking around the mill. This was a lie. — What did the man look like?

Captain Steen who as a listener was sitting in the courtroom, slipped out. He walked with shaky steps down the road. His teeth chattered, and cold drops of sweat trickled from his brow.

…

What did he look like? — Well, Braaten had only seen him in the dark, so he couldn't give a more detailed description of the man's appearance.

The police in any case wanted to try to find a trace of "the mysterious looking man."

Besides, they had looked for Hall's body these two days in vain. The boat had been brought into the bay behind the sandbank by backwater.

Fløiberg was sitting alone in the garden room when the captain came back from court. He heard him go up the steps and into his bedroom.

Fløiberg was much too occupied with other thoughts to be able to notice that there was something wrong with the captain. He goes through the newspapers that he tosses helter-skelter over the table. Tries to assume a calm, indifferent mien. But it doesn't work. — Doesn't Jenny have something to say to him before he leaves. He has just told Magda Naadheim that he intends to leave tomorrow. — All at once he looks toward the door. A little click. He listens. And suddenly he again begins to read the newspapers, but without grasping a single word of what he is reading. — Hush! — there she comes. … But it was just Miss Naadheim who came in and started to look after various things. She wanted to arrive in time so as to be present in case something should happen. She smelled bad weather.

Finally, Jenny comes from the dining room, walks over to the piano, flips through sheets of music, looks around – and now and then casts a scornful, indifferent glance at Fløiberg. Then she goes over and picks up a newspaper and sits down nonchalantly in an armchair, close to Fløiberg. He read in Jenny's face the bitter opposite of what he had imagined. He felt crushed.

"Isn't there something about yourself in the papers today, Mr. Fløiberg?" asked Jenny with suppressed laughter.

"No," answered Fløiberg, tense and indifferent. He became so bewildered that he forgot to remain quiet and cast a hushing, superior glance at her as he recently had been wont to do.

"It is surely also very long ago the newspapers had the honor of mentioning you. Have you perhsps forever withdrawn to the peace of the private life? — Isn't it about two years since this famous notice stood in a newspaper about student Falk Fløiberg having returned from Africa?"

"Yes," answered Fløiberg in a thick, mushy voice. He again forgot to keep quiet, but read more and more zealously.

Jenny gloated amusingly at his embarrassment. "Oh yes! So quickly perishes this world's splendor. Especially when ones mundane splendor is not so great. — Well, well. — You can of course console yourself with having once been famous in your life. I beg your pardon! — Two times. Just think, two times! It wasn't my intention to pretend I didn't remember your biography that was in a newspaper that time you matriculated. I know that by heart – exactly! To this day still. How did it sound? (Thinks it over and can hardly keep from laughing.) — If only I could remember the beginning. — Yes — "Among" — it began with "among" — yes, now I have it! "Among this year's students there is a young man who already has an unbelievable story behind himself" … And so on —

So the story goes. "You probably ought to get yourself a new copy of this document soon?" she said finally as she threw herself backwards and laughed wildly. She jumped in her seat and died laughing. "For the old one is surely as worn out as an inherited Bible in a Haugian house. That has indeed been your calling card for four entire years. And a calling card ought not to be old and worn out. Get several hundred copies while you're at it."

Fløiberg sat as if on embers and hid behind the newspaper.

"But you're thinking of surprising the world yet again. That treatise on plant bacteria – signed F. F. – that almost sounds like B.B." She said it with an ironically serious mien. But then she burst into a violent laughter again. "Here one can in truth with a little rewriting of the script say: the letter gives life; but the spirit kills it."

Then Fløiberg got up and went out through the veranda door. She jumped up too and shouted after him in the door: "Tell about your experiences one more time! There's only one more day that we have a living hero among us."

She closed the door and exclaimed pathetically: "He wandered among us!"

Miss Naadheim folded her hands together. "I would never have believed that you could be so shamefully ill-bred, Jenny?"

"Once I probably had to have been shamefully ill-bred, I too." The hard-heartedness in her voice was too striking. "Did you see how sincerely inviting he looked to tease now? He is sometimes irresistible in that direction."

"So he is not irresistible in other directions any more?"

"I hate him! God, how I hate him!"

She looks out through the window. Miss Naadheim sits down and watches her in slience.

After a long pause Jenny finally says: "it's so strange to think about."

"What is it that's so strange to think about, my child?" asks Miss Naadheim with motherly tenderness.

Jenny embraces her and hides her face in her breast. Wasn't it refreshing for the old maid's desirous, but renouncing heart to be able to be a refuge for a daughterly trust. "What is it that is so strange to think about, my Jen?"

"That I shall share a room with Pastor Richter. This tall, hard man!" Jenny said. She chuckled a bit wildly and unrestrained … There was morphine in her laughter. — She felt relief – for a while.

"You are a naughty girl. God knows, what kind of pastor's wife will become of you?" Magda was motherly concerned.

"Oh, I can almost swoon when I think about it! I don't know how I'll manage."

"You know, Jenny, you can turn to me assured and confidentially with all your anxieties."

"To you who has never been married?" Jenny said with a deep, chuckling laughter, since she thought she wanted to collapse under the rising unease.

"Hm – I am in any case old and ex…! You always come out with your sarcasm. This darned poisoning is truly not the very best thing in this world."

Jenny was in the middle of the spiritual process wherein the deep, smoldering pain and desperation in silence decompose and then at blazing speed consumes the happy element – a sudden, violent explosion and then everything is quiet again.

She again went over to the window and looked out. She didn't want to answer Magda's many questions any more. She couldn't. She felt that her voice would betray her.

But then she couldn't be silent any longer. "I feeel so sad."

Magda took her around the neck. "What's the matter with you, Jenny?"

Jenny burst into tears and clung to Magda. "I feel such a frightening emptiness in me."

"Is it especially now you feel it?"

"Yes."

"Do you maybe regret that you were so bad to Fløiberg?"

"Yes. That was so dumb, so badly done by me." She cried sorely and bitterly. "Oh, I will never again be happy if he leaves me in this way."

"You know what! I'm afraid you still love him. Without you knowing it yourself. But I must most earnestly beg you by all means to try to be sensible. Haven't you yet gotten to know that fellow?"

"Yes, God knows, I love him! I can't help it. I have never loved anyone else."

It was as if the words broke through a stone arch under which for a long time she had in vain tried to suppress them. Words imprisoned that suddenly flew into the air! She had to listen to their sound in the air. Were they still so strongly alive?! Not once in the quiet, wakeful nights had she dared to let them pass over her lips; they darted like electric sparks from her nerves that she had constantly tried to round off so as to chase them back.

…

"Listen – your father is coming down. Hurry out so he doesn't see you this way!" They both walked out through the dining room.

… The captain looked in the mirror, but recoiled as if he had seen an appalling sight. His lips were blue and had feverishly quivering twitches, and his eyes had something dementedly wooden and staring about themselves. His neck had shrunk deeper down between his shoulders.

He cursed this meaningless and ghastly instance that had led him there on that very night. All of a sudden he had to hold his head with both hands; his poor brain tried in vain to work its way out of this terrible enigma. Why hadn't the occasion allowed him to wait one more night? And yet he had waited a hundred times to the next night. — And when all is said and done, had he really wanted to set fire to the mill? Hardly. The previous night he had been in the woods to get his things; but he hadn't dared take them along when there was such strong moonlight.

But now – if only night would come! He was going to get them and burn them up, even if the sun and hell both began to shine during the night.

What if Fløiberg was missing his large, broad-brimmed hat! – As bad luck would have it, he carelessly had put it on that fateful night.

And what if someone found the things in the woods!

…

He went into the dining room and drank a couple glasses of cognac. Well, that helped. He could almost think clearly and calmly. "One doesn't absolutely have to think the worst either now. — And I who am innocent? Am I a coward?! — That's ludicrous too. He managed a real smile.

Then he gritted his teeth, clenched his fists as in a brutal fight with himself: "I'm going to subdue this damned cowardice." He shook his fists. Damn it all that twinges of remorse shouldn't be granted him honorably and fully. Even if he had had a real crime to deal with?

He felt a pleasant impenitence seep into himself, and his nerves seemed to be satisfied with that.

He wanted to go out in the garden, but met Fløiberg in the door.

Fløiberg was somewhat pale and had taken on a rare calm. He was full of a need to abstain from using controlled, malicious words – if only he could meet Jenny, and preferably now right away while he was in a good mood.

The captain stopped. It shouldn't look like he was fleeing from people. But this time Fløiberg saw right away something unusual had befallen the captain.

Both wanted to get away from each other as quickly as possible; but they were both as if nailed fast.

"It looks as if there'll be bad weather," the captain said.

"Yes, it looks like that."

"You've been at court today? — Well, how is it going with Braaten I wonder?"

"He's still denying." The captain cleared his throat and looked around nervously. He couldn't get around to telling about the strange looking man Braaten had mentioned – although he knew it would be best for himself if he in simple innocence – and preferably with surprise and noise at reporting the news – told it.

"But if he really is guilty," the captain said, "and nevertheless continues to deny, and avoids his punishment – what then?"

"Hm, as far as punishment is concerned it makes no difference. He'll get enough of that anyways."

The captain looked doubtful at him: "What kind of punishment?"

"Punishment by suspicion," answered Fløiberg as he glanced at the captain, not because he had any suspicion whatsoever that he had anything to do with the fire at the mill, but from the sheer need to look impertinently brazen at people – so necessary he even wanted to let his bad mood affect the captain. "Punishment by suspicion," Fløiberg repeated. "No one will accuse him directly. He just has to meet people's long, suspicious glances. He must guess what others are thinking. And compare his crime with that of the thought – the conscience's uncurtailed purpose – and not with short, stunted words – or this punishment by immersion for several years."

The captain listened to the inflection. Was it the usual verbiage of Fløiberg when he was in a bad mood – or was it an inquisitorial gimlet?

He went in to fill his pipe; but his fingers were tender and trembled. His pipe fell repeatedly to the floor.

XIV

The same afternoon Fløiberg is sitting in his room.

There's a knock on the door. Jenny comes in, slowly and apprehensive, so she is almost on the way to withdrawing. "I wanted to ask your forgiveness …" Her voice had a faltering sound.

Fløiberg got up and said in a polite, but cold tone: "Please, just come in." She stood there a while silent and at a loss. Fløiberg enjoyed this pause with a malicious smile. He had succeeded in maintaining his mood from the morning on in full. "What is it the young lady is so grieved by?"

"You must forgive me, Fløiberg. I wasn't myself when I spoke to you that way this morning." She looked down at the sofa and hid her face.

"I think you were in high spirits then." — Again pause.

"You have never wanted to understand me," she said with immediate, loving sadness she couldn't nor wouldn't hide.

"Let us not be sentimental, young lady! We have certainly understood each other very well. And therefore also understood how to hurt each other in such a superb way, as we have been able to do for mutual edification. But now we must one day stop this game. One cannot just live off the pleasures of pouting either."

He walked back and forth and smiled triumphantly. "Besides I want to thank you so much for the fun."

"We mustn't part in this way, Fløiberg! You don't know what you're doing if you leave without – without saying a single friendly word to me."

"Yes, I know it. You see, I dare like to think I am doing you a favor by leaving. And preferably in this way. You can then more uninterrupted and with a better conscience enter the spiritual chamber."

Then Jenny got up, ripped the ring off her finger and threw it down on the floor.

Fløiberg looked at her a little surprised; but he controlled himself. "You are throwing away happiness." He stood and looked with an ashamed glance down at the ring. "Richter's ring. — Ach! — Mein Liebchen, was villst du noch mehr, he said!" He took the ring up and looked at it.

"You are thus not as you try to be." Now she looked at him. But this time he couldn't look her straight in the face. He turned away. The incomparable sincerity in her look had paralyzed him. She bent down again and wept quietly.

Finally, Fløiberg went and put his hand on her shoulder and said: "Jenny, I want to forgive you."

"You want to!" She looked up and took hold of his hand. Fløiberg made a deprecating gesture and said: "I only want to forgive you. And I hope that you will forget everything there has been between the two of us."

But she held him firmly and whispered agitated: "And then say something good and friendly to me! Say Jenny once more! — You just said it now. It was so lovely to hear. As in the old days when you said Jenny to me."

…

They held eath other's hands for a long time and seemed at a loss. A miraculous flow of blood made her tremble when she felt how he warmly and fervently squeezed her hand.

Finally Jenny said: "Let me have the ring."

"I'm happy that you have become sensible again." His lips quivered.

"You see, I want to throw it into the stove," she said.

"That you may not do until you have gotten sensible again."

She grabbed both his hands. "I don't want to hear about sense. Oh, can't you either refrain from talking about this disgusting sense! — Let me have the ring!" She again looked at him.

"You can't have it."

Both of their voices quivered. They became hot in their cheeks, didn't look each other in the eyes, but struggled for the ring. Jenny got a good hold on him. They slid more and more into each other's arms. She closed her eyes, and he kissed her.

And they kissed each other again and again and with vehement and insatiable passion. They pressed themselves intensely into each other as if they were afraid there might be a space between them.

She held both her hands around his neck and looked into his eyes: "I am so heartfelt happy! Never have I been as happy as now. I can hardly believe that it is me holding you around the neck – and that it is you looking at me like this. … Like this!"

"Can you remember, Jenny, that Sunday afternoon we were sitting down in the garden room? The two of us, entirely alone?"

"Yes, I remember as if it were now. Then we also began to fight for the ring. — I wanted you to take it by force."

"I did that too."

"Yes, you did. And then I came to sit on your lap just as now. — But with the big difference that you didn't kiss me that time."

"Nor you me."

She pressed herself anxiously in to him, kissed him for a long time, as if to assure herself that it was now happening. "I was waiting for you to do it," she said.

"And I was waiting for you to do it, Fløiberg answered.

"And then there was no kiss," she sighed as she with all her body tried to cover him under herself. — "It is said that between the beaker and the mouth there is always room for a viper."

The great and bitter pains remain like shadows to pursue a person throughout life. For long periods it can seem as if they have disappeared completely and for good; but just as one has sat down in joy's bewitching lap, they pop up suddenly – as bloodthirsty creditors who want to remind you they are keeping an eye on you, and that they will never renounce their demands for retribution and avenging justice.

…

"You must not look so hateful! You make me miserable. — What is it you're thinking about?" she said when she saw his face was beginning to turn dark and cold.

He answered a little haltingly: "About your girlfriend. How such a person can be loathesome. She was herself unsuccessful, but nevertheless wanted to have something to do with love. She made intrigues." — "Ugh, what a repulsive, clammy creature she was!"

"Yes, but I assure you I didn't care the least about what she said."

"That could well be. But she always made expressions that she was carrying secrets between you and Richter. And it was this abominable mien I couldn't stand seeing. As she always gave the appearance of having something especially important, a valuable secret to report."

His voice quivered. He got up, He had to exhale. Jenny took him around the neck and said: "But I loved only you. That you must be able to understand."

"Yes, I understood that. But you didn't have the means to renounce Richter's flirtation. You wanted to have sunshine and love from all sides. You lay like an affectionate cat."

"But don't you remember how horrible you yourself could be to me? You forced, forced me to be together with Richter. And you even kept yourself cruelly and strictly away from me. I cried many times. For it hurt me so."

"It hurt you, yes. I knew that. That's exactly why I acted thus. I suffered myself at it. But I couldn't let it be. And yet I was bloodthirsty to hurt you, regardless of the means."

With anxious suspense she observed all the alarming dark lines in his face, tried to brush them away – like a mother watching over her sick child. "I almost didn't sleep for several nights when I heard last year that you were going to come here again. I had a fever."

"But then the illusion burst when you got to see me in reality. Ragged and worn out like a toothless, wingless devil. And then you were busy traveling to Kristiania."

"Now I'm getting mad at you when you talk like that. — God knows, I loved you even more then. I knew that it was my fault you had gotten into that state. I wanted to talk with you, but you always turned aside. I wanted to be friendly and kind toward you, but you rejected everything. — It was Richter and Papa who forced me to travel. And then I couldn't do anything else. Papa wanted to have you alone to himself. He couldn't be happy without you. — Oh, how you have been cruel to me, dear Fløiberg! You haven't spoken a single word to me, since I came home this spring. Well, we haven't spoken with each other for almost four years."

After a little pause Fløiberg put his hands around her waist and said as he looked at her with an odd look: "Jenny, may I be allowed to kiss you? Just this one and only time?"

She took a couple steps back. Agitated and alarmed.

"Well. As you wish," he said.

His look was wild.

He laughed maliciously and walked out. His steps and his posture staggered when he headed for the woods.

XV

Now he had gotten a breeze on his forehead. For several hours he roamed around and over the wooded hills. He was on the way home. How he would now make her happy! He would carry her in his arms. Everything would be forgotten. To see her radiant eyes when she hurries into her arms now, thrilled and rueful! — His chest bulged as he floated over the path.

With a pounding heart he stepped into the garden room. He met only Miss Naadheim. She looked critically at him – as the one who is in on the situation, she smiled so sweetly and beguiling. For every time she had the opportunity to satisfy Fløiberg, she forgot all the troubles she had steadily been exposed to on his part. And then Fløiberg usually found a bottle of wine in his room.

"Jenny has been looking for you; but now she has surely taken a stroll."

"Where is the captain?"

Magda suddenly became serious, coughed a couple times and looked mysterious. She peeked into the garden room to assure herself that there was no one who could hear her. Then she took a couple deep, agitated breaths, and after still another dozen extra preparations all of which were calculated to make him inquisitive, she asked as she grasped him by the arm: "Tell me …," she had to take yet another look around the room, "tell me, are you missing a hat?"

"A hat?" He looked astonished at her and loosened his arm from her hand with a certain disgust. "Have you perhaps found it?"

"It was found." She pressed her mouth together and breathed through her nose quite frightfully. "Promise me now solemnly and sacredly that what I tell you in no way must come further. — Yes, you see, Ole has found it. And you know what?"

"Really?"

"In the woods on the other side of the river."

"What are you saying?!"

"Ole was there this afternoon to chop up some windfallen trees. And while he is trimming branches from a large spruce tree, he catches sight of your hat. And do you know what else there was? — Peter's crofter's jacket – and a pair of the captain's stockings!"

Fløiberg suppressed his agitation. "And how can this be connected?"

Magda rolled her lips together and prepared in an exciting, dramatic pause to dish out the actual essence. "Ole's and my opinion is that the captain the other evening stood disguised outside the windows at the doctor's. He couldn't leave it at that to try to get a glimpse of his cousin anyway. You know that the captain has recently shown that he wished to be reconciled with his cousin. And that evening he went alone and began to regret not going with the rest of us. For it's so strange when one goes with such uncertainty and doesn't know what to do.

Yes, wasn't it like a bad omen, this here?

The captain is standing like a ghost and looking in through the window, and just then the whole mill is in flames. For he presumably stood there at just that moment."

"That could well be possible," Fløiberg said.

XVI

It is already late in the afternoon. The captain is atanding down on the shore. For the third time he begins to follow the narrow path that leads along the sand bank and up to the river bridge. But when he has come close to it, he says for the nth untold time that of course he must wait until nightfall. He turns the same way back. Stops. Suppose someone hits on walking in the woods this evening! No, I have to go there immediately. Immediately! He turns around and hurries along the uneven path. The sweat pours down his forehead, and his heart pounds so violently that it whistles in his ears. He was again nearby the bridge. — "I didn't set fire to the mill." He stops again suddenly. "I didn't set fire to the mill. I am as innocent as a lamb. — I think the devil incarnate is riding me!" He seems to wake up from a bad dream.

… There had been quite a fresh breeze inside the fjord the entire afternoon. People who were dragging for Hall's body had had to go ashore.

The wind howls in the treetops and blows a few flute sounds in the thin, dry twigs on the shore – brushes so ticklingly cool over the captain's feverish forehead. Snarling curly waves shine in the fjord. The monstrous clouds that for a long time have hovered over the sea way out, push forward with brutal force, so it whistles and shrieks in the air that plunders thick specks of water and rolls and piles them inside the fjord and far up onto the sandbank, out on the point of which the captain now stands and seeks relief and diversion in the powerful spectacle, the sea in uproar, which like a powerful giant in a death struggle shows the whites of its eyes. The moonlight breaks through the cracks in the rolling cloud masses that glitter and shine like bluish icebergs.

"I didn't set fire to the mill."

The storm howls and frets and groans in the swaying woods.

The captain plays like a wild Indian. When the breakers roll back, he runs after them – only in wild flight to head upward again when a new billow hurries after him at ferocious speed and in his disappointment at already being outside its reach spits some water after himself.

He walks along the bay. He has become bolder and wilder in his game. He dances and fences and becomes intoxicated in the diversion; half demented he whimpers into the storm:

High foams the sea in white billows
and underneath overhanging streams of water,
while prayers from the heart follow a sigh from the sea,
I cool my forehead.
resonant sighs the blood in swelling veins,
and the eyes in flight wheedle the gods,
who chase among stars with flashes of white tears
and proclaim peace to me.

He follows a breaker all the way down. A swell more powerful than all the others comes snarling and seems to scrape all the way down to the bottom. He stands in a position to set off, but waits until it's right at his heels. But this time he makes a mistake. The swell summons its last powers and wolfs him down, lifts and hurls him upside down, and right away he feels something – like a heavy bundle – roll over himself – he crawls up with all his strength, blows water out of his mouth and nose, but stumbles and falls again. And finally he lurches over the heavy bundle, while the sea rolls back again. His hand glides over something that feels like a face. He casts a demented, staring glance at it. The cold, open eyes look at him. The shine from the moon penetrates deeply into the gray, transparent corpse skin.

…

Fløiberg was sitting on the edge of the bed holding a water compress on the captain's forehead, when the doctor and Jenny stepped in.

"It's the death-eyes! Can't you take him away? — Don't you see that it's shining through the skin?"

...

They had understood right away that it was the sight of Hall's corpse that had brought him into this state. People walked down to the shore and found the corpse.

No, the doctor said, it was nothing dangerous.

How refreshing it was for Jenny to see Fløiberg's mild and devoted, somewhat weak expression on his face. This expression she had never seen before. There was something so strange about it, and yet it struck her right away that this was the way he really was. It was his so far hidden essence that now revealed itself. The pliant and tender.

Behind the doctor's back he grasped her hand and kissed it tenderly. Such a pleasant calm and security Jenny hadn't felt in a long time. Calm weather after thunder and lightning, while pearls of water hang and drip down from the trees' branches.

...

Finally the captain fell asleep.

"You can go," the doctor said. "Tomorrow the captain will be completely well again." As an experienced doctor he wanted to prevent Jenny and Fløiberg from hearing what the captain would possibly say in his sleep.

They walk down to the sea and sit down on a bench in the pavillion. The storm sighs in the tall trees and bushes. The driving clouds are gaudy in the moonlight, and the breakers' snarling can be heard down on the sandbank.

She lies in his arms and feels how fervently firmly he holds her in his grasp. She breathes in confident abandonment.

"Falk, you must never again make me sad!" He didn't answer, but the trembling closeness whereby he pressed her into his chest, spoke more than words.

Yet, the heavy, melancholy expression on his face wouldn't recede.

"There is something oppressing you," she says as she holds him around the neck and looks into his eyes. "I see it. — Dear Falk, you mustn't make me anxious!"

"No, my dear, little, beautiful Jenny! — It's not to make you anxious!"

"There is something wrong with you. Tell me what it is!"

"It's just a bad thought, a bad hallucination bothering me."

Jenny started up and pressed her hands to her chest: "Is it something with Papa?"

"No – no! Absolutely not!" he pulled her down onto his lap. "No, far from it! — It is a friend of mine – not a friend actually, but an acquaintance of mine I'm thinking about. It doesn't even concern me, but anyway I can't refrain from thinking about it."

Why in the world couldn't he refrain from arousing this suspicion in her. Perhaps the whole thing was only a colossal misunderstanding by him, about the captain and the fire at the mill. And yet he couldn't get rid of this thought. It slipped with its long, ghostlike arms into him everywhere – pressed and squeezed him together with its green, sharp claws.

"Jenny, don't be so sad! — Be happy! — Don't you see how happy I am?"

But she heard the false joy in his voice as it strained in his smile.

"You know what most alarms me?" she said. "It is because I see you are sad and in despair, in spite of you being so reluctant to hurt me. Before it was willingly you treated me so awfully. Then you were burning with vengefulness. But now – now you frighten me against your will, Falk. — Is it dangerous? — Speak frankly!"

"How beautiful you are, Jenny! — Sleep peacefully." He kissed her with tears in his eyes.

XVII

During the quiet nights the senses play their most beautiful and richest music. Darkness deadens the light's pallid thoughts; but the bashful longings smolder up from their hiding place. The night owl's eyes sparkle, the preditors' passion swells in their limbs. The juices trickle from the full pores and flow like titillating pearls on the nerves …

*   *

*

Jenny gets out of bed. For the third time. She has lain awake for a couple hours. Yet something very frightful must have happened to him. And who knows: maybe he breaks down sooner than someone else? She knew him …

She opens the door. It's completely dark in the large dance hall. She stands still – and then takes a couple steps across the floor. It's as if everything reels for her. Trembling and shaking now and then go through her body. She can't understand it; she's not freezing. But nevertheless she can hardly stand on her legs. Her eyes tear up quite involuntarily.

She didn't think about what she suspected. She thought convincing herself that he hadn't gone and done away with himself. But she – her body – suspected something else.

She stands at his door and listens through the keyhole – hears that he every so often breathes out a heavy sigh and says one or other disconnected word aloud. — Several times she is about to withdraw, yet remains standing.

Then she hears that he quickly gets out of bed, jangles some keys and opens his suitcase.

It is of course the revolver he wants to get hold of, she thinks. (Had she in haste given herself time to reflect, she would have perceived that she forced herself to think that way.)

She knocks a couple times on the door. Silence. Knocks again.

"Who is it?" he whispers through the keyhole.

"It's Jenny. I'm so afraid for you."

He presses her to himself as her young, warm breasts fill his arms. He uncovers her breast and kisses it.

It is the sunrise of life.

JOANNIS SCHEFFERI
ARGENTORATENSIS

LAPPONIA

Id est,

REGIONIS LAPPONUM
ET GENTIS NOVA ET
VERISSIMA DESCRIPTIO.

In qua multa

De origine, superstitione, sacris magicis,
victu, cultu, negotiis Lapponum, item Animalium, me-
tallorumque indole, quæ in terris eorum proveniunt,
hactenus incognita

Produntur, & eiconibus adjectis cum cura illustrantur.

FRANCOFURTI
Ex Officina CHRISTIANI WOLFFII
Typis JOANNIS ANDREÆ.
ANNO M. DC. LXXIII.

XVIII

At nine in the morning the captain is standing in his office. He smiles. He can hardly keep from laughing. It forces its way up from him spontaneously. He has just spoken with the sheriff on the telephone. People have, he related, found a diary in Hall's pocket. And as far as one could see there was a lot that was compromising for Braaten. They were now going to try to confront him with the body. Besides he has been very dispirited and nervous. Presumably he would soon confess.

… The captain smiled. That he could have been so dumb – to imagine pure nothingness. "And I who am not guilty!"

Oh, so safe he felt now! He was standing by the window. The rays of the sun played on his smiling face. He is released from a grave full of ghosts snapping at his ill-fated soul.

The blood runs quicker and quicker through his veins. "Ah, it is as if my heart wants to jump for joy!" He holds his chest and breathes vehemently, jumps around and hops in the air, really jumps. Swirls around on his heels. And laughs like a little child, while tears of joy trickle down over his cheeks. He tries to put on a calm and serious air, but immediately bursts again into a convulsive laughter. — "I am a lucky happy child — God's child! — Devil's child! — I am whose child I want to be! I am happy." He giggles and slaps his thighs. "Now I'll ride up on the mountain's tallest peak. Hip, hip! Hip indeed, old nag! The high mountain air will fill my lungs, and the sun's gentlest rays will shine on me!" — He strokes his face and breathes illustratively. — "What difference does it make if they find the clothes? Which they'll never do. There isn't a soul who can hit on thinking that it is I who was outside. The clothes were naturally stolen here at the estate, they'll say." He didn't know about Ole's find in the woods.

He walked into the living room. Here he met Jenny.

"You look so hearty and buoyant now, Papa."

"You think so, my girl? — Good business, Mother! That's the best medicine. Sold shares and earned a lot of money, Mother. Got the word by phone just now. — What? — I should probably buy you a new hat, you wench? — And hold a booming wedding? You naughty child. Well, well, damn, get married even if tomorrow !"

She took him around the neck and could hardly keep from crying. "Look, Papa!" She held her right hand out.

The captain shoots up and looks open-mouthed at her. "What? — What? — What in the world? — What is this supposed to mean?!"

Jenny burst into tears. "I can't - I don't want to get married to Richter; never in the world can I do it!?"

He took a couple steps back and looked at her from top to toe. "Does Richter know about this?"

"Well? — What? —."

"I am engaged to Fløiberg," she finally managed to stammer.

The captain was on the verge of losing his breath. "Engaged to Fløiberg! — Lord help me — by God, have you gone crazy!"

Jenny clings to him. "Dear, dear Papa! I love him. I can't help it. I have never loved anyone else."

The captain snorted and chortled. "Love Fløiberg! Good Lord, you're funny. — So you love Fløiberg! No, God bless me if I've ever heard anything like that!" He laughed so extremely derisively as if he had his deceased wife before himself. "Yessiree! I will with pleasure buy you a hurdy-gurdy and a deck of cards so you two can play and prophesy for people. For it is surely the intent that you are going to live too?"

"Can't you be a little more serious?"

"More serious?! I don't think it fits the situation." He stared hard at her.

"Papa! — It depends on who laughs last."

She walked out.

*   *

*

Fløiberg had been awakened by a large, well-rounded life. Now he felt related to everything alive. For long periods his strengths wept from privation, frittered away in the wasting winds, the seven lean winds that seemed to want to tear up the last threads which connected him to the living life. Now he stood firmly on the good earth. He enjoyed this new, brave feeling, so blessedly free of abnormal feelings and forbidding brutality. Now he had the means to clear the way of everything that had hindered him from helping himself to life's great dishes that lay in abundance around him. The feeling of abundance – spiritual affluence had swelled up in him. His courage grew up from reconciliation with life.

He walked down into the garden room and met the captain, right after Jenny had walked out.

The captain had prepared himself to give him a proper dressing down, and waited impatiently for Fløiberg to punch a hole in his gall bladder. Besides Fløiberg had no idea what had happened between Jenny and her father.

"You mustn't misunderstand me, captain. But I am forced to ask you a question that is not pleasant. — Where were you that night when you disguised yourself – that night when the mill burned down?"

The captain turned white as a corpse. He had difficulty breathing. He couldn't get out a word.

"Maybe it's best that we go into the office." The captain staggered in and Fløiberg followed after.

"I – I didn't se… set fire to the mill!" the captain finally groaned forth.

"But why were you disguised that evening? — Why did you hide your clothing in the woods?"

"Say, for God's sake, where you got to know this?"

"I will tell you when you have told me the full truth."

Then the captain burst into a vehement weeping, a weeping so unpleasant, as only an older, hardened man's weeping can be. And meanwhile he explained the whole truth. The words twisted and struggled up from his throat; they sank down and popped up again and he gave a hoarse shriek from himself. "Oh, I've been a wretched person!"

The abscess had gotten a cut. The tear became larger and larger. His whole life's misery flowed forth in front of him …

His unpleasant sobbing had gradually changed into a mild, muffled weeping.

"You won't of course disclose a word of what I have confided to you?"

That far Fløiberg had not thought. He couldn't answer. The question turned everything upside down for him.

The captain looked frightened at him. "You'll say nothing. You would never think of making me distressed?!" — He suddenly gets an inspiration. "You love Jenny of course? — And she loves you. She has just told me that herself. Take her! Ask of me anything you want! You can do with me whatever you want. Just don't betray me!"

The captain had said what Fløiberg was afraid of letting his thinking take notice of. The captain's words had suddenly opened a rotten dam that glistened from black slime and clammy, green snake eyes.

"And I should walk around conscious that I have gotten Jenny by means of despicable, loathesome villainy!"

Now he was convinced that the captain's account was a lie from beginning to end and that no one other than the captain could be the arsonist.

If only he had never gotten to hear a word of this captain's frightful story! His desperation couldn't have been greater even if he himself had been the arsonist.

He jumped up in a rage. "God knows, I'll shoot both Jenny and myself if there isn't ...."

The telephone rings.

Braaten has confessed.

…

Jenny stands on the steps. She cannot believe her own eyes. Her father and Fløiberg are walking arm in arm over the fields and take the path that leads through the woods up to the crest of a hill …

Heavily and groaning a little, the captain walks up over the hills, supported on Fløiberg's arm.

The woods rest under a veil of fine, light green color. Now and then quivering bird wings whistle in the air up toward the day's rising sun.

They sit down each on his own tree trunk by the side of the road. There's a little dam after the downpour this morning. The pearls of water still hang on the spruce needles and sparkle and blink in the sun's rays that break through some grizzled, woolen clouds and dapple the soft greensward with marvelously beautiful and mild colored features.

The captain's narrowed eyes follow a couple insects stuck on the water surface and furrow and shred the shiny surface.

They sat quietly.

Finally the captain said: "It's so remarkable that I invariably must think about it." He spoke a little out of breath and then fell silent. He was fumbling for words … "I remember that night. That horrible night. I felt so strange. I thought that all of a sudden I was snatched away from my home, away from people I had grown up together with from childhood on … Now too, I feel strange in relation to that existence I have led until now. But with the big difference that I have now drawn closer to life. Everything is so new and yet so – so – well, I don't know; I am like a person who after a long time absence has come to his childhood home. It is new because he has jumped over a long and bleak chapter in his life – and then suddenly stands on the ground of his only happy memories. He stands half way between dream and reality."

He got up.

"Then there was something I wanted to have said to you, Fløiberg." He cleared his throat, but couldn't hold his tears back. "I beseech you that you mustn't misunderstand me there, that I am afraid that you will betray my secret. I understand very well that you dread taking Jenny for fear that she will become yours by virtue of despicable means. Yes, I beseech you not to take it that way. Jenny's and my happiness in life depends now on you. And your own as well. I stand in great obligation to you. And my greatest joy would be to be able to do something good for you."

Of what use is it to call someone to account for sin? thought Fløiberg, but he didn't say it …

Down on the fields Jenny came toward them. She was dressed in light colors. Her young bosom grew from expectation.

Matti Aikio (1872-1929), a Sámi from Karasjok, Finnmark, Norway, was one of the world's first indigenous writers. His 1904 novel *King Ahab – or Falk and Jenny* was published in Copenhagen. His first Norwegian novel *In Reindeer Hide* came out in 1906 four years before Johan Turi's *An Account of the Sámi*. Turi wrote in Sámi (with some help from Emilie Demant), whereas Aikio, who did not begin studying Norwegian formally until he was eighteen, spent most of the rest of his relatively short life in Oslo writing in Norwegian. He wrote articles for newspapers and Christmas magazines as well as eight books of which six were novels. He was writing during a period of harsh assimilation and social Darwinism. His books were popular among Norwegians who were interested in the exotic people up north, but they were less successful among his own people, in part because he saw that the best way forward for the Sámi was to learn the majority language which was tantamount to his supporting assimilation.

The illustrations between the chapters of *King Ahab* – copperplate engravings – are taken from Johannes Schefferus' 1673 book *Lapponia* about the Sámi, their history and culture. Schefferus (1621-79) from Strasbourg was appointed professor at Uppsala University in 1648. His book was intended to counter rumors the Swedish army was employing Sámi magic, i.e. shamanism, on the European battlefields. One of Schefferus' main informants was Olaus Sirma (1650-1719), a Sámi theological student at Uppsala. From Sirma Schefferus got two yoik texts "Moarsi fávrott" and "Guldnasaš" about a man's love for his woman who is not present. Hence, they are the beginning of Sámi literature. For more information see Harald Gaski's *In the Shadow of the Midnight Sun* (Davvi girji 1996).

Dr. Elina Helander-Renvall from Ohcejohka, Finland is a Sámi scholar with many articles and books to her credit. Her research areas include Sámi customary law, traditional knowledge, traditional cultures and llifestyles of the Arctic and sustainable development. She also happens to be an excellent artist and produced the painting on this book's cover. For more of her work go to siida@samimuseum.fi

Gunnar Gjengset is a Norwegian scholar, an aphorist and a playwright. He received his fil. dr. from the University of Umeå in Sweden with a dissertation omn Matti Aikio. Gjengset earlier published *Dobbelt hjemløs*, a biography of Aikio. He is also the biographer of Gustav Vigeland, the famous Norwegian sculptor.

John Weinstock, Ph.D. from the University of Wisconsin in Madison, taught Scandinavian languages, Sámi culture and Wagner's operas at the University of Texas at Austin for many years. He has translated a number of works from Norwegian and Swedish and published numerous articles on the Sámi and their origins.